PRAISE FOR LAKE OF DESTINY

"Delightful, charming, and heartwarming!"

—*NEW YORK TIMES* BESTSELLING AUTHOR
WENDY HIGGINS

*"I adored every page . . .Beautifully written, perfectly paced
with traces of magical realism.*

—AWARD-WINNING AUTHOR ERIN CASHMAN

*"Well-written, well-crafted, well-paced and full of
heart. . . . So much charm it's magical!"*

—*BOOKGEEK*

*"Martina Boone's gorgeous storytelling enthralled me from
start to finish. The plot is captivating, whimsical, and full of
surprises that kept me turning the pages."*

—*SINCERELY KARENJO*

*"I loved this!!! It reminds me of a Nora Roberts series, The
Gallaghers of Ardmore . . . but a Scottish version with men
in kilts!"*

—*TWO CHICKS ON BOOKS*

"*Outlander-Lite Meets Gilmore Girls in Scotland. This is a story that sucked me in from the start and didn't let go until I'd laughed, shed a few tears and worked up an appetite. Fast. Fun. Romantic. Read it!*"

—JENUINE CUPCAKES

"*This book had it all, romance, fantasy, folklore, drama, and emotional family issues. It's a great story and I enjoyed every minute.*"

—LINDA R.

"*It was funny, sad and uplifting and just brings you in for a warm embrace. I look forward to more from this amazing writer.*"

—JAN JANUS

"*Full of myths, legends, and life. The plot is good, the characters are great, and I couldn't put it down. When is the next book?*"

—CHERYL BOND

"*This was so good I'll be reading it again. A wonderful story . . . with a touch of the fantasy of Brigadoon. I had to read it in one sitting.*"

—DEBRA CHASE

PRAISE FOR COMPULSION

"Skillfully blends rich magic and folklore with adventure, sweeping romance, and hidden treasure . . . An impressive start to the Heirs of Watson Island series."

—PUBLISHER'S WEEKLY

"Eight Beaufort is so swoon-worthy that it's ridiculous. Move over Four, Eight is here to stay!"

—RT BOOK REVIEWS, RT EDITORS BEST BOOKS OF 2014

"Boone's Southern Gothic certainly delivers a compelling mystery about feuding families and buried secrets, not to mention a steamy romance."

—BOOKLIST

"Even the villains and not-likable characters were just so engrossing. I have to say I've already put the sequel on my TBR shelf."

—USA TODAY

"This Southern gothic mixes dark spirits, romance, feuding families and ancient curses into the perfect potion."

—JUSTINE MAGAZINE

WELCOME HOME

—Historic Romance of the Celtic Legends—

Also By Martina Boone

Adult Fiction:

Lake of Destiny: A Celtic Legends Novel

Bell of Eternity: A Celtic Legends Novel

Magic of Winter: A Celtic Legends Novel

Young Adult Fiction:

Compulsion

Persuasion

Illusion

WELCOME HOME

—Historic Romance of the Celtic Legends—

MARTINA BOONE

MAYFAIR
PUBLISHING

MAYFAIR
PUBLISHING

712 H Street NE, Suite 1014,
Washington, DC 20002
First Mayfair Publishing edition April 2017
Copyright © 2018 by Martina Boone

Jacket design by Kalen O'Donnell
Interior Design by Rachel & Joel Greene
Published in the United States of America
ISBN 978-1-946773-18-0 (trade paperback))

To all those who love wild, beautiful places
with a little Celtic magic.

WELCOME HOME

—Historic Romance of the Celtic Legends—

Celtic Romance

"Faeries, come take me out of this dull world,
For I would ride with you upon the wind,
Run on the top of the disheveled tide,
And dance upon the mountains like a flame."

W. B. YEATS
THE LAND OF HEART'S DESIRE

THE HISTORIC LANDSCAPES OF Ireland, Scotland, Wales, and Cornwall are steeped in thousands of years of myth, tragedy, and heroism. The landscape is wild and beautiful, the people are kind, fierce, tenacious, loyal, and romantically tragic—the very stuff of which heroes are made. For a writer, this is gold, but it's also food for the soul, renewal in a world where it's sometimes hard to find a hero.

Legend, history, food, and music—almost as much as the settings themselves—are at the core of each of my books in the Celtic Legends Collection.

Although my fiction is all set in the present, there is a bit of historical backdrop to every book, as well as a legend or snippet of folklore that adds to an element of suspense. (And of course, there is romance, some of which comes from the fact that my heroes tend to be modern men in kilts.)

Lake of Destiny, set in the Scottish Highlands, features Rob Roy MacGregor, the Children of the Mist, and the feud between the MacGregors and MacLarens. There's also the legendary tradition of "Sighting," which occurs on Beltane morning when the veil between worlds is thin.

Bell of Eternity, set on a fictional version of St. Michael's Mount in Cornwall, involves the escape of Charles II, the forces of Oliver Cromwell, and a lost abbey bell with mystical powers, along with the legendary romance of Tristan and Isolde and the lifesaving traditions on the island that go back all the way to the early saints.

Magic of Winter takes us to the Highlands and the "Sighting" again, but it's focused more on the heroic women of the Highlands, those who managed to defend and feed their families and tend the livestock and farms when their men were off raiding and playing at war. Like Mary Queen of Scots, they were often used as pawns, and sometimes their stories ended tragically. But like Mary, so many showed dignity, defiance, and determination to survive.

Echo of Glory (2018) covers the consequences of imbalances of power, both in the modern world and in the past, touching on one of the many dark periods of Irish history with the Dursey Island massacre and the O'Sullivan death march. It also brings in the Irish Brigades. Oh, and Vikings.

Heart of Legend (2018) is set in Wales near the Devil's Kitchen and Caernarfon, and it deals with the tragic history of Owen Glendower, the Defender, the last Welshman to hold the title "Prince of Wales," whom Shakespeare described as a man ruled by emotion and magic.

Because readers often email me about the recipes or songs or legends I mention, or ask about the history that serves as a backdrop, I want to share some of what lies behind the scenes, the personalities and the complex, human motivations.

Mostly, what follows in this book provides an overview of the historic struggles between England, Scotland, and Ireland seen through the lens of the biggest personalities, the most beloved, hated, and tragic heroes and heroines, including Rob Roy MacGregor, Mary Queen of Scots, and Bonnie Prince Charlie. But there are lesser known stories, too. People such as:

- Alastair MacGregor, whose exploits led to the MacGregors becoming "the Children of the Mist,"

- Flora MacDonald, who whisked Bonnie Prince Charlie away to Skye dressed as a maid,

- Donal Cam O'Sullivan, the Prince of Beare, who led a guerrilla war against Queen Elizabeth's army that helped the other Gaelic Irish lords nearly bankrupt the English treasury,

- Morty Óg O'Sullivan, Captain of the Wild Geese, who fought a rear-guard action after the tragedy of the Battle of Culloden with his Irish Brigade so that Bonnie Prince Charlie could escape,

- Viscount "Bonnie" Dundee, who gathered support for the first Jacobite resistance and fought so valiantly that it was said he had made a pact with the devil and couldn't be killed with lead.

These are some of the longer stories, but along the way and woven in between are the backdrops and the events that shaped the nations—and the reasons why those events occurred. There are also smaller tidbits of personalities tucked in there, the tragic stories of what Henry VIII's quest for new wives did to the daughters of the wives he discarded, and thereby to three different countries, for example. This includes Elizabeth's sexual assault, Mary's very public eleven-month-long false pregnancy, the tragedy of Lady Jane Grey, and more.

The stories are organized loosely in relationship to the settings of my books, but like the turns of the Celtic wheel that shift from light to darkness and back to light, each is a small piece in a larger story. They mirror and build upon each other, and even after tragedy, death carries a wistful whiff of hope. You can read them in any order by jumping around in the table of contents. Within the major stories, I've tried to embed enough information to make the history understandable, but important points are also covered in between in more chronological order.

There's no such thing as pure history. That is especially true here. I'm presenting a mixture of personality, psychology, history, legend, and personal opinion. Again, it's meant as an overview for those who love the tragic heroes and heroines of the Celtic nations and their struggles, and for those who find that the usual histories so often leave out the hopes, dreams, and vices of the players, thereby making the bare facts dull and incomprehensible.

In 55,000 words, the history I offer up can't be

comprehensive. And sometimes I have to tackle difficult issues in a relatively short space, which can't possibly hit all the critical points. The struggle between Catholics and Protestants, and between different types of Protestants, is a huge backdrop to why so many of these wars and struggles took place. Discussing this can't be avoided, but for the big players on the stage, those in power, nothing that happened was ever really about religion—or any one thing. Their motivations were always mixed and fluid.

The vast majority of both Catholics and Protestants involved in these struggles were just ordinary people trying to feed their families and live their lives in as godly a manner as they could. The same is true for the Gaelic Irish in Ireland, the Highland clans in Scotland, and virtually everyone else. They were defending their homes and families. On the English side, most were following orders and trying to save their livelihoods because they had families to support. So many of the problems, too, were caused by splits and conflicting motivations within different factions. You can't ever accurately say "the Scots" or "the Irish," or even "the English," as though interests within those countries were all aligned. Partly this is because of natural differences that grew from territorial, political, cultural, and religious allegiances, but partly it's because the English Crown had discovered early on that seeding their own supporters in Scotland, Wales, Ireland, and Cornwall made it easier to control those territories.

Even the idea of supporting one's family often had a different meaning back then than the way we think of it today. Wealth and power were built over generations, and the higher one flew, the more dangerous it was to lose what one had. Enemies a family made along the way were always waiting in the wings to pick over the bones after a fall. Families therefore often hedged their bets, keeping a father on one side and a son on the other or placing sons on either side of a war or rebellion.

Wealth came with privilege—and also with the power of life and death over literally thousands of people. There was an additional price tag, one wherein many of the wealthy and powerful removed themselves emotionally from the people beneath them. *People* too easily became a commodity, pieces on a chess board, their lives and lands something to be moved aside as necessary to achieve a goal. This is still too often true.

Just as there are today, there were unscrupulous, self-serving people on both sides of every conflict I describe in the following pages. You'll probably detect some tone in my descriptions of the leaders whose actions resulted in the suffering of hundreds, if not thousands or tens of thousands, of others. I'm not a fan, for example, of either Henry VIII or Oliver Cromwell, nor do I much love any king or queen. If I were writing a pure academic history, I would make a greater effort to keep you from seeing my own biases, but I know myself well enough to acknowledge that I have an affinity for the underdog and against those who behave cruelly and with self-serving interest. This can't help coloring my opinions, and even by picking and choosing what facts and whose stories I include or leave out, I'm necessarily shaping how the history and personalities come through in these pages.

In short, while I'm being as accurate as I can, I'm also creating a story with selected historical events. I hope it will be a taking-off point for you to go and find out more, to form your own opinion.

History *is* opinion. That's what we aren't taught often enough these days. The common narrative is written by the winner, with dissenting opinions tainted by the bitterness of the losers. Without fresh facts, historians may restore a bit of color here, a new perspective there, but what really happened is lost somewhere in between the brushstrokes. To piece it together accurately, we'd need many more perspectives from across the spectrum of people who were affected, and far greater insight into the hundreds of additional decisions and motivations that took place in the white space between the handwriting that issued orders.

If there's a pattern to be seen in any of this history, it's that any imbalance of power—as my characters discover in *Echo of Glory*—is inherently dangerous. The individuals I've described have families and causes, and they found themselves teetering at the very small tip of political pyramids—doing their best not to topple off as the entire structure was constantly bombarded from England. All families had in their midst weak men and brave, cruel men and kind, stupid men and brilliant ones. Some of the deeds were dastardly—there's no excusing that, and I'm not trying to do so. I do try to strike a balance where the facts support it.

The lessons of history are complicated. We all love the legends that have been passed down through the ages about the heroes whom history has not forgotten. If I'm trying to achieve one thing here, it's to show the history behind those legends, to illustrate that history is not just about battles and documents. It's about people—it's a tapestry of lives, loves, fears, families, loyalties, personal advancement, personal failure, greed. Emotion. Human frailty. Humanity. And yes, all too often *in*humanity is woven in there along with everything else.

Again, feel free to use the table of contents to jump around to what captures your imagination. In addition to the legends and historical overviews, I've included a selection of songs that were written about the history in these pages, as well as some recipes that I hope will provide more insight and enjoyment. I occasionally send out recipes, music, and snippets of history and story in my newsletters, too, while I'm researching a new novel or when a book has recently been published. Please do sign up on my website if you're interested. The information for how to do that, along with a free offer for an upcoming book, is located at the back.

Rob Roy's Grave

*"Many miles away
there's a shadow on the door
of a cottage on the shore
of a dark Scottish lake."*

SIR WALTER SCOTT

Y EARS AGO, ON A SPARKLING blue afternoon, I was
driving in the Scottish Highlands when I passed a
rusting black-and-white road sign pointing to Rob Roy
MacGregor's grave. Now, being a sucker for Scottish history,
Sir Walter Scott, and Liam Neeson in a kilt (not necessarily
in that order), I had to take the detour. And I fell utterly in
love with the Balquhidder Glen.

The location itself was beautiful, of course, in that wild
way of Scottish glens with steep-sided, heather-covered
braes and lochs glittering silver beneath an endless sky, but
it also had an aura of something magical. Something *more*.

Sometime in the eighth or ninth century, St. Angus reportedly came to the glen and described it as one of the places that the native Celts considered "thin," where the demarcation between Heaven (or the Otherworld) and Earth was more permeable than elsewhere. He spent the rest of his life there and built a church near the spot where the Victorian church still stands, alongside the ruins of another stone church and the cemetery where Rob Roy MacGregor lies buried.

Rob Roy was a MacGregor chief, a hero to many, an outlaw to the English and many Scots. He was the subject of a novel written about him while he was still alive—one of the first instances of a literary celebrity in his own lifetime. He's been written about ever since, with perhaps the best known examples from Sir Walter Scott and the film *Rob Roy* starring Liam Neeson. I'll delve more deeply into Rob Roy in upcoming chapters, but while Rob's history permeates the Balquhidder glen and still brings in many—if not most—of the tourists who visit the area, his burial in the graveyard there is lately somewhat controversial.

The first clan chiefs in the area were MacLarens, but they lost their chief in the sixteenth century and officially became "chiefless and landless." It wasn't until 1957 that a successful petition was put forth in the Court of Lyon to restore a rightful chief. That chief, the MacLaren, had a home in the glen of Balquhidder, and he wasn't best pleased by all the attention still given to Robert Roy MacGregor.

The Gaels, the Celtic people of Scotland, Ireland, Wales, and Cornwall, are a passionate folk. Their memories are long, and their loves and hatreds both run deep. And historically, the MacLarens have no cause to be friends with the MacGregors.

The enmity between the clans goes back to a disagreement in 1558 when a MacGregor raid in the Balquhidder glen, perhaps instigated by the Campbells, saw the death of the MacLaren and many of his kinsmen. Chiefless, the MacLarens were pushed out of their ancestral lands, some of which have since been occupied by MacGregors. More on this later, too.

An inscription placed in the Balquhidder kirk in the nineteenth century read:

IN MEMORIAM OF THE
CLAN LAURIN ANCIENTLY THE
ALLODIAN INHABITANTS OF
BALQUHIDDER AND STRATHEARN
THE CHIEF OF WHOM

IN THE DECREPITUDE
OF OLD AGE TOGETHER WITH
HIS AGED AND INFIRM ADHERENTS,
THEIR WIVES AND CHILDREN,
THE WIDOWS
OF THE DEPARTED KINDRED,
ALL WERE DESTROYED IN THE
SILENT MID-NIGHT HOUR
BY FIRE AND SWORD
BY THE HANDS OF A BANDITTI OF
INCENDIARISTS FROM GLENDOCHART.

A.D. 1558

As I said, memories are long. The new twentieth century MacLaren chief not only disliked the fact that the public sees Rob Roy as a hero, he also cast doubt on where Rob is buried.

A fictionalized aftermath of that feud between MacLarens and MacGregors features in both *Lake of Destiny* and *Magic of Winter*, where in my version of the glen both families coexist, along with Stewarts and many others, and where disagreements still collect loyalty along clan lines. Following these lines is complicated, given centuries of marriages, but also because the MacGregors weren't always allowed to use their name. For nearly 200 years, the very name MacGregor (including Gregor) was banned by the Crown and Parliament.

The words "MacGregor Despite Them" are engraved on the tombstone at the head of the grave where Rob Roy lies buried beside his wife and two of his sons. More about this later, too. But it was these words, along with the scenery, that first fascinated me as I drove almost by accident into the Balquhidder glen all those years ago.

The grave is romantic enough, but to complete the picture, it lies—near the Victorian church alongside the beautiful ruin of an old stone church, which was likely built on top of the one from which St. Angus preached. It was here, at this second church, that a soberly Presbyterian minister, the Reverend Robert Kirk, preached in the seventeenth century. Since this was in the midst of the Protestant Reformation and the Bible was, for the first time, being made accessible to the common people, he raced to be one of the first to translate portions into Gaelic. He went to London to supervise the printing of Bishop Bedell's *Gaelic Bible*, and was himself responsible for translating the *Psalms of David in Metre*.

But according to legend—and his own writings—in between his Sunday sermons and other duties, the Reverend Kirk would sometimes wander outside in his nightclothes and venture away into the faery world of wonder and magic.

Years later, as the legend goes, he was taken back to that Otherworld to become the chaplain to the Fairy Queen, and he never returned.

He collected his own faery encounters, along with those from his neighbors, into a manuscript that he worked on until his death. A century later, Sir Walter Scott (who also made Rob Roy MacGregor a household name) published these stories in a book titled *The Secret Commonwealth or an Essay on the Nature and Actions of the Subterranean (and for the most part) Invisible People heretofore going under the names of Fauns, and Fairies, or the like, among the Low Country Scots as described by those who have second sight.* Most scholars of folklore consider this to be one of the crucial and authoritative collections on faery folklore. Folklorist (and beloved author of all those rainbow colors of Fairy Tales) Andrew Lang published a second version of this in the late nineteenth century, called *The Secret Commonwealth of Elves, Fauns and Fairies.* I spent hours and hours poring over Lang's books as a teenager and young adult.

As if all this wouldn't have been enough to fire my imagination, before leaving the Balquhidder glen, I also had an encounter with a flock of meandering sheep, a lonely horse bit the side mirror of my rental car when I tried to stop petting him, and a shaggy Highland bull charged over to lick my camera lens while I was trying to take his picture. (I still have the photo of his tongue.) Add to that a lovely meal and an hour-long conversation with a Scottish nationalist who passionately and patiently explained why Scotland never should have been—and still shouldn't be—subservient to, or lumped together with, England, and it was a day I've never forgotten.

I knew I would write about the glen someday, but I also knew it would be a story about modern feuds with ancient roots. I needed a way to bring in that mystical aspect that both St. Angus and Robert Kirk found in the glen, that idea that there are things beyond our human sight and understanding, things about fate and destiny and magic we can't always see with our eyes but must believe with our hearts.

To this end, I had to make some changes to the setting for *Lake of Destiny*. Because the place has changed some since the first time that I visited, and because the legend of the "Sighting" on Beltane morning is purely a figment of my imagination based on a range of ancient Celtic folklore, mythology, and traditions, I wanted to make it clear that my Balwhither isn't exactly the one you'll find when you wander off the highway. For this reason, I chose to use the name Balwhither for my fictional setting. It's the phonetic spelling of Balquhidder, anyway, and it's also one of the spellings Robert Louis Stephenson uses in his books. (Although, quite literally in the space of a few paragraphs in *David Balfour*, he spells Balquhidder in three different ways.)

Both in my fiction and in real life, the glen is near Loch Katrine, not far from the famous Loch Lomond. It lies a short distance into the Highlands beyond Callander and the Trossachs, partway between Stirling and Glasgow. Not far away, one can visit Stirling Castle and the battlefield at Bannockburn where, in 1314, Robert the Bruce and William Wallace—of Braveheart fame—along with a force of less than 10,000 Scots defeated King Edward II and his army of 20,000 English, leading ultimately to victory in the First War of Scottish Independence.

The Scots—and the Irish and Welsh, for that matter— have a habit of snatching victory from much larger foes. It's one of the things that makes their history so fascinating and heartbreaking.

Entering the glen, you can follow the single-track road along first Loch Voile and then past the much smaller Loch Doine. Because of the legend of the "Sighting," I renamed these Loch Fàil and Loch Daoine. Between them, there's a narrow peninsula where the legend of the "Sighting" is engraved on a stone:

ON THE BRIGHT DAY
IN THE MORNING DEW
TO THE PURE OF HEART
THE LAKE OF DESTINY
WILL REVEAL THE TRUE LOVE WHO
WILL WARM THE WINTER OF YOUR LIFE
AND THE LAKE OF ENCHANTMENT
WILL TURN SIGHT TO TRUTH.

The "bright day" is Beltane, one of the four cusps of the year that hang between seasons, and in some places in the Gaelic countries there was a tradition of washing the face in the morning dew of Beltane to usher in spring and bring prosperity after a long, hard winter. On Beltane, there were also bonfires and various rites, including gifts given to the fae and wishes left on trees. All of this is woven into the "Sighting," but it's the effect of knowing who you are meant to love that caught at me when conceiving the book.

How do you live your life if you already know who you will end up loving? What if you don't *want* to marry that person? To have that sort of life? How does such foreknowledge affect you when you meet the person whose face you already recognize?

In a place where feuds already ran deep, I could envision this leading to so many bad choices, problems, and secrets.

I do so love fictional secrets . . .

Beyond Loch Doine, the real Robert Roy MacGregor had a homestead. The road stops here, at Inverlochlarig, where my fictional Connal MacGregor now has a manor house. But continuing down the glen from here and crossing over the mountain, one would arrive at Loch Katrine.

Rob Roy was born across the mountain near this much larger lake. It was also along Loch Katrine where, at Brenachyle in 1753, Bonnie Prince Charlie's friend and trusted aid, the Lieutenant Colonel Doctor Archibald Cameron, was captured in the last and final gasp of the Jacobite Risings.

The "Bonnie" Prince, the heir to the ousted Stuart line, was the son of King James, who had been deposed for being Catholic, and too much of an absolute monarch, and replaced with the Protestant William of Orange from Holland, who was married to James' daughter Mary. I'll get to much more about the whys and wherefores of the Jacobite Risings later, but for now it's only important to know that there were three major attempts to restore the Stuart kings. Rob Roy MacGregor's father fought in the first, in 1688, and was imprisoned for treason afterward. Rob Roy himself fought in the Rising of 1715 at the age of 18, and he—in turn—was imprisoned for that. The Rising in 1745 ended in the tragedy of the Battle of Culloden, where Bonnie Prince Charlie's army was slaughtered and the prince escaped purely due to the bravery of the Highlanders and the men of the Irish Brigade who laid down their lives to provide him cover. The Skye Boat song records the journey in which Flora MacDonald snuck him away to Skye disguised as a maid so he could later return to France. A legend in Ireland claims he spent one night on Dursey Island in Cork, before the swashbuckling local O'Sullivan Beare chief, Irish patriot and smuggler, Morty Óg O'Sullivan, whisked him away in the ship he used to sneak deserters from the British army over to France to fight in the Irish Brigades. (More about Morty later and in *Echo of Glory*.)

But the Risings weren't meant to end in 1745. There was a reason that Archibald Cameron came back to Loch Katrine in 1753, which was that he was back to retrieve the gold that had been earmarked to pay for the Jacobite Rising of '45. The gold had been lost, and—some say—with it the hopes of the Jacobite cause. Legends claim the search for the gold continued, and in fact continues still. It is possible, though, that it was intercepted by the English at the time. It's not a small sum—today it would be worth close to $14,000,000.

Archibald was also there to organize a new plot to assassinate George II and other members of the English royal family, paving the way for Prince Charles to return. Presumably, paying for this was why the gold was needed. That, however, is also a story for another time, one I haven't written yet, so stay tuned for that.

The gold wasn't found, and the assassination plot didn't go anywhere, either. Cameron was betrayed by the notorious "Pickle the Spy" and taken to the Tower of London, where he was hanged, drawn, and quartered, the last Jacobite executed on Tower Hill. With him ended all hope of restoring the Stuart dynasty.

Balquhidder is a wonderful place for walking, settling in at a charming bed and breakfast, having a delicious tea in the afternoon, or just driving through on a windy afternoon when the sunlight and the honey scent of heather sink into your skin.

And when you turn your head just so, your imagination can play tricks. The fae vanish in the shadows of the trees, and blurred bits of tartan plaid disappear into the mists of the Highland braes, like the long-vanished and nameless men of the clan MacGregor.

Highland Rogues

"My name is not spoken," she replied
with a great deal of haughtiness.
"More than a hundred years it has not gone
upon men's tongues, save for a blink.
I am nameless like the Folk of Peace."

ROBERT LOUIS STEVENSON
CATRIONA

ONNAL MACGREGOR, THE TROUBLED HERO of *Lake of
Destiny,* is a descendent of Robert Roy MacGregor.
And like Rob Roy, when he's being hunted, he retreats to the
glen of his ancestors for refuge. In Connal's case, he's doing
all he can to shelter his disfigured daughter from the
paparazzi following the death of her mother, a famous
actress, in an alcohol-involved accident. But because Connal
is himself a well-known actor, protecting Moira means that
he has to change his name from the one he used on the

screen. In *Lake of Destiny*, in other words, Connal is going *back* to the name MacGregor. I did that as an echo of history.

The MacGregors are arguably both the most maligned and most glorified of the Highland clans. Most probably, to paraphrase Jane Austen, they deserve neither such praise nor such censure. They had a fine advocate in Sir Walter Scott, but they also had great enemies, the MacLarens, the Colquhouns, and, most importantly, the Campbells among them. And with the enmity of the Campbells came the enmity of the Scottish—and eventually—the English Kings.

The MacGregors were outlawed for nearly 200 years, the men allowed to be hunted and massacred like animals, their lands confiscated, their very name prohibited on pain of death. That's the reason the tombstone at the head of the grave where Rob Roy, his wife, and one of his sons, are buried, proclaims that he was a "MacGregor Despite Them." Because the use of the MacGregor name was prohibited during his lifetime, he used his mother's Campbell surname until he himself became an outlaw. At that point, already pursued by the authorities, he used MacGregor as a challenge and signal of defiance.

Rob Roy's exploits became so famous that a book published about him in 1723 ultimately prompted King

George I to send an emissary to Scotland to meet with him, leading to new adventures. Sir Walter Scott wrote *Rob Roy* based on that book in 1817, and the 1723 book is usually credited to the work of Daniel Defoe, but there is no official author on the early copies. The National Library of Scotland has it listed by an anonymous author under the title *The Highland rogue: or, the memorable actions of the celebrated Robert Mac-gregor, commonly called Rob-Roy.*

I'll get to more about Rob Roy specifically in the next section, but the importance of Scott's story is that it not only helped Rob Roy obtain a pardon and live out his latter days in the Balquhidder glen, it also helped shape the way the entire MacGregor clan is remembered. Given the history I'm about to tell, that becomes critical. It's a great example of the pen being mightier than the sword.

And the truth is, applying common sense to the situation, they can't have been as bad as they've been painted by many because, given the weight of the laws and the power of the punishments levied against them, they wouldn't have survived without allies.

It comes down to this: while the Highland clans were bound by powerful ties of family and fealty, there were many different branches. The entire MacGregor clan was the subject of the laws meting out their persecution, but it was chiefly a single branch of one family that brought about their eventual downfall.

Just as James Graham, the Duke of Montrose, was the villain of Rob Roy's story, the Campbells of Glen Orchy were the force that brought down the MacGregors before Rob Roy was ever born. It is this feud that led to the MacGregor clan becoming the "Children of the Mist."

Beloved Gregor

"Ba hu, ba hu, little orphan,
you are only young yet;
But I fear the day will never come that
you will avenge your father."

Marion Campbell MacGregor
"Griogal Cridhe"

THE MACGREGOR CLAN WASN'T large as far as clans went, but it was one of the oldest in the Highlands. Their very motto of "My Race is Royal" went back to the oldest of the Gaelic chiefships, and at one point they had owned nearly half of Scotland. In a bit of irony—given Rob Roy's later use of the Campbell name—their problems started with a dispute with one particular branch of the Campbell clan that had a seat at Glen Orchy.

The Campbells, a powerful clan, and the MacGregors had long been uneasy allies. They fought together for Robert the Bruce, and bled together on the battlefields at

Bannockburn and Stirling Bridge, but the Campbells came out ahead when it came to rewards. It was a Campbell who ended up married to the Bruce's sister, and their son became the first Earl of Atholl. Well placed now, when the MacGregors supported the Lord of the Isles in a dispute a little later, Bruce's son, David II, gave a fair bit of land that had once belonged to the MacGregors to the Campbells, including the barony of Loch Awe. Over the next centuries, the Campbell power grew even further, and they received a number of additional titles, becoming the Earls of Argyll as well as Atholl, although the Atholl title soon passed to the Murrays and it was the Earl of Argyll who became the Campbell chief.

With the dominion of their land given over to the Campbells, the MacGregors now went from being their equals to being their vassals, bound to serve them in military service, sometimes in the course of this waging war against neighboring clans in an odd mixture of English feudalism and Highland clan allegiances. But still, the MacGregors and Campbells remained on fairly good terms. They intermarried, fostered each other's children, and stood surety for each other's oaths.

Then, for a period, the fortunes of the Campbells of

Glen Orchy waned. Their lands dwindled. The MacGregors were pressed into the service of Iain Campbell of Cawdor by the Campbell, the Earl of Argyll, and various legal means were taken to further reduce the lands and standing of the MacGregors.

By early in the sixteenth century, the Campbells of Glen Orchy and Strachur were both determined to rebuild and grow their holdings. Then Iain MacGregor of Glen Strae died without children in 1519, which left a power vacuum. This created a period of instability in which varying MacGregor factions squabbled. The Campbells stepped in, asserted some creative muscle, and came out much to their own advantage with a claim to the MacGregor lands at Glen Strae.

We now come to Colin Campbell, known as "Grey Colin," who inherited the Campbell estates at Glen Orchy. And he, and later his son "Black Duncan of the Cowl," went on a major offensive to rebuild the Campbell of Orchy fortunes using any means at their disposal, most of them—though not all—legal, if highly unscrupulous. Systematically, they pushed out or impoverished neighboring families and replenished their own estates.

The MacGregors, while generally known to be good

businessmen, were, in contrast to this sort of quiet, patient Campbell scheming, of more forthright, stubborn, and fiercely independent natures. In some cases, this played right into the hands of the Campbells, because lands could—and often did—become forfeit as the result of disputes. Someone with connections could game the system, in other words, by pushing someone into armed conflict, having them commit an offense against you, and then petitioning for their lands as reparation. The Campbells had those connections, and they used them.

Over the course of some years of systematic pressure, Grey Colin managed to maneuver the MacGregors into a position more and more within his control. The feud, which had started relatively small in Grey Colin's area, spread gradually into Lochaber, Atholl, Strathearn, Menteith, and the Lennox, involving almost all the great families in Argyll and Perthshire. It cut off trade and travel and became a great disruption overall.

Colin pressed the MacGregors tighter and tighter. Not only did they lose land to him directly, but he also squeezed the Earl of Argyll into returning them back into his own service as vassals. This time, however, it was not simply fealty that bound them. The Earl of Argyll gave Colin the legal overlordship of the remaining MacGregor homelands, with effective control of the main MacGregor Glen Strae seat. This left them powerless to stand against Colin, regardless of what he asked them to do. Otherwise, they would have risked losing their last remaining stronghold.

The middle part of the sixteenth century was a bit rocky in Scotland—as it was elsewhere, come to that. Henry VIII had decided he needed a new wife (more about this later) so he had dumped the Catholic Church, along with the power of the pope, and set himself up as the head of the Church of England. This coincided with Protestantism breaking out in Europe through the influence of Martin Luther and John Calvin, which for the first time gave common people—those who didn't read Latin, though not the masses who couldn't read at all—access to the Bible and separated religion from the corruption that had crept into the Catholic Church.

The people of Scotland, who had all been Catholic up until now, started to accept these Reformed doctrines—with quite a bit of help from Henry VIII, who wasn't thrilled about having a Catholic country, with allegiances to the pope and to Catholic France, along his most vulnerable border. He'd only recently fought a fresh war with James V, the

Scottish king, and he'd gotten a good reminder of how fiercely the Scots could fight.

To make matters even more complicated, right after that war with Henry, James V had died, leaving a six-day-old daughter as his only heir. Mary Queen of Scots obviously couldn't rule herself, so her French (and Catholic) mother, together with a succession of powerful lords, were the ones actually in charge.

Henry had realized it would be a wonderful plan to get rid of a separate Scottish monarchy altogether, and what the English hadn't managed to accomplish since before Robert the Bruce, he decided he could accomplish through marriage. To this end, he proposed a wedding between the new Queen of Scots and his own son Edward. Mary had only to allow herself (or rather to have her regents make her) to agree to be basically brought up as English, and Protestant, and to come and live in England when she was ten years old.

There were some Protestant and pro-English factions who thought this was a good idea, but a lot of other people didn't agree, so Scotland plunged into civil war. Into this, Grey Colin and his son Black Duncan waded with skill and great political savvy.

The Campbells were Protestant. The MacGregors—most of them—were still Catholics. In essence, they were on opposite sides of a war for much of the next few years.

Mary had been whisked off to France and married to the heir to the French throne, and even managed to, very briefly, become queen of France before her husband died. For years, French soldiers had helped to stabilize things for her in Scotland.

This wasn't entirely from the goodness of their hearts. Thanks to his very public matrimonial machinations with the your-mother-and-I-were-never-technically-married-at-all and the other your-mother-committed-treason-so-I-chopped-off-her-head thing, Henry had managed to make *both* his daughters, Mary and Elizabeth, technically illegitimate, and though he later jumped through some legal hoops to fix it, he left a loophole that made Mary Stuart a legitimate contender to be not only queen of Scotland, but also queen of England and Ireland in her own right.

Mary's claim to the throne wasn't lost on the king of France. He lost no time once Henry was gone in declaring Mary, along with his own son, as the rightful queen and king of England, Ireland, and Scotland. But Mary wasn't old enough to rule yet, and by the time she was, her French husband had already died. With less at stake, and a religious uprising on their hands at home, the French couldn't do much to help Mary at home.

In 1561, Mary came home to Scotland, just turned eighteen and a brand new widow, to finally claim her throne. England had seen a quick succession of monarchs since Henry VIII. Edward VI had lasted six years, and since he'd been a young boy when Henry died, he'd had self-serving regents governing for him most of the time. He'd been followed by Lady Jane Grey (more later about poor Jane), who was queen for only nine days, then by Bloody Mary, who was Catholic and did her best in her short time as queen to stamp out some of that pesky Protestantism by burning people at the stake. Now, finally, there was Elizabeth II, who was just coming into power when Mary arrived on Scottish soil.

Elizabeth was Protestant. Again. And seeing both Mary and Scotland as a threat to her crown, her country, and her faith, she began quietly stoking Protestant and pro-England, pro-Unification fires across the Scottish border.

War, always simmering in the background, erupted in full force. An alliance of pro-Catholic, pro-"Auld (French) Alliance," and/or loyalist Stuart supporters fought against newly reformed pro-English Scottish Protestants, who had taken control during the time regents ruled in Mary's stead while she lived in France. John Knox, a fiery preacher supported by Elizabeth, basically said Mary was the devil and did his best to swing the tide of public sentiment against Mary and her supporters.

But Grey Colin Campbell of Glen Orchy played politics very well.

The staunchly Protestant Campbells, and most especially the Earl of Argyll, had been fighting on the pro-Protestant, pro-English, pro-United-Britain side of the wars in Scotland, not to mention meddling deeply in Irish politics on behalf of England, and they now had to face a reckoning when Mary managed to ward off all challengers and settled herself firmly on the throne of Scotland. Grey Colin presented himself at court, penitent, swore fealty to her, made some fairly easy guarantees, and off he went home again with the queen's good graces—and her ear for future MacGregor disputes.

An opportunity arose almost immediately. Two MacGregors killed some Campbells.

Gregor Roy MacGregor had just come of age and become the new chief of the Clan MacGregor. Now Grey Colin gave him a choice. He could hand over the two men who had killed the Campbells and agree to some "unspecified legal restrictions" or he would have to give up his lands at Glen Strae.

In effect, the choice was this: Gregor could become homeless, or he could be powerless.

Gregor Roy answered Colin's ultimatum by attacking a Campbell convoy, setting off a period of intense fighting that lasted eight years. There was one hiatus in the hostilities between 1565 and 1567, and in that period, Gregor Roy married Colin's niece—which made what happened next still more horrible even than it would otherwise have been.

In 1570, Colin Campbell swept in and took Gregor Roy captive, holding him prisoner for eight months before winning a judgment from a jury of mostly Campbell supporters, which gave him the right to execute Gregor Roy.

Gregor's wife, Marion, heavily pregnant with the couple's second child, was present at the execution. Afterward, she wrote one of the most beautiful laments in Scottish literature about her feelings. (There's an English translation of *Griogal Cridhe*, "Dearest Gregor," included in the songs section of this book.)

Now, into this environment was born Alastair MacGregor of Glen Strae, who grew up in the home of a stepfather chosen for his mother by her Campbell father, a woman who lamented his father's death and hated and bitterly blamed her own Campbell relations for their treachery in bringing about his death. Grey Colin and his son Black Duncan controlled Alastair's rightful family seat, and the power, dignity, and ability of the MacGregor family to live as free men was virtually broken.

By now, the quarrel had largely passed from Colin to Duncan, who would become the first Baronet of Glenorchy. Duncan was even smarter and more unscrupulous than his father. He pushed the MacGregors. Hard. And the harder they pushed him back, the more he used his connections to turn the law against all MacGregors.

Dispossessed of their lands, their livestock, their very identities, the MacGregors scraped out a living any way they could. This wasn't always strictly peacefully or honestly. Their very reputation came to be steeped in "lawlessness," and they became adept at vanishing "into the mist," protected by the rugged terrain of the Highlands as well as, clearly, the loyalty of many people who could have turned them in. Their very reputation for lawlessness was fostered by the Campbells, though, and yet they were still Campbell vassals.

There began a long period where they balanced on the knife-edge, falling in and out of favor with the Campbells while navigating complicated business dealings, land issues, and political pressures. At various points, the Campbells would either leave them alone or hunt them and kill them with impunity. The MacGregors would periodically retaliate, or instigate.

To survive, under Alastair MacGregor, the MacGregors developed an even stronger reputation for raiding.

Now, many of the Highland clans were warlike and independent at the time, so raiding wasn't unusual. Family fortunes, countries, and monarchies had always—up until then—been forged by taking something at sword's point that belonged to someone else. Furthermore, under the Highland system, one didn't always have a choice about whether or not to participate in a raid. If one owed loyalty to someone else, if the land you farmed was within their territory, or if you fell within their clan—or your clan was a vassal of some other lord—you might not have the option to refuse.

For whatever reason, survival, loyalty, opportunity—or a combination of the above—while other clans were also raiding, the MacGregors became so adept at stealing the cattle of their enemies that it has been suggested that the term "blackmail" or "black meal" is derived from the idea that if you befriended the MacGregors, or paid them enough, they would leave your cattle or property alone. (In truth, "black rent" and "black taxes" were known by many different terms and collected by many different families—in Scotland, Ireland, and elsewhere.)

Here, though, we come back to the MacGregor raid on the MacLarens of Balquhidder.

Indisputable facts concerning this story are very scant. It happened in 1558, and in the course of the raid, eighteen MacLaren men were killed. Their families were either killed or dispossessed, and MacGregors took control of their homes and land. Again, this was not unusual at the time—it had certainly happened to the MacGregors more than once. But the MacGregors had no political clout at this point, no protection—in theory. Yet, until nearly fifty years later, in 1603, no complaint was made against them for these murders, and by the time it was first mentioned, they were already being tried for other offenses. Even then, while they were pronounced guilty on other charges, they were cleared of crimes against the MacLarens.

The lack of complaint about the MacGregor raids prior to 1603 certainly wasn't for lack of opportunity. In 1593, for example, after a MacGregor had killed a royal forester while poaching on royal land, the situation escalated to the point where Mary Queen of Scots herself gave the order for her soldiers to pursue the MacGregors by "fire and sword," which meant that they could be killed with impunity and their homes and livestock burned. Again, there is no mention of the MacLaren massacre as justification for this order.

And the MacGregors somehow survived—which suggests they had more allies than is generally reported.

But then . . . along came a new problem. There was the matter of the Colquhouns and the massacre of Glen Fruin.

Massacre of Glen Fruin

"But doom'd and devoted by vassal and lord,
MacGregor has still both his heart and his sword!"

SIR WALTER SCOTT
"MACGREGOR'S GATHERING"

OF THIS PARTICULAR STORY, there are multiple versions. In the MacGregor-friendly version, two MacGregor men on a journey asked for food and shelter from the clan Colquhoun at Glen Fruin near modern Glasgow in 1603. The Colquhouns turned them away, and the MacGregor men, by now both cold and hungry, killed a sheep which, being a rare "black" sheep, led to its absence being almost immediately discovered by its owner. The two MacGregor men were summarily executed. And in retaliation—allegedly—the MacGregor chief mustered men and went to avenge his two lost clansmen and the lack of hospitality given to them.

That's one version.

Another possible interpretation is that the MacGregors had come to collect the "black" sheep (which could be plural) that were the sixteenth century equivalent of a protection racket the MacGregors had gotten very skilled at running. Many of the transactions people made at the time involved the exchange of livestock, and this was especially true in terms of the "black rent" or "black tax" that families like the MacGregors charged to leave someone's property and livestock unmolested.

A third version, one even less friendly to the MacGregors, is far more complicated.

The MacGregors had a history of raiding on Colquhoun land. They weren't alone in raiding or causing trouble in the Highlands. As I've already pointed out, raiding your neighbors was a pretty popular pastime back then, for one thing, and for another, in many cases, such "trouble" was a question not just of fighting for survival, but of who was loyal to the person sitting on the throne, whether they were Catholic or Protestant—and which particular flavor of Protestant—and their general alliances and debts of duty owed to more powerful lords and clans who routinely stole land from each other. Due to the very complex system of clanship and allegiance, along with a slew of other reasons, in 1587, the Scottish Parliament had enacted the Act of General Ban, which held lords accountable for their vassals and the actions of the people living on their lands. In effect, this made the Earl of Argyll—despite his having given the Campbell of Glen Orchy control of the MacGregor family seat at Glen Strae—responsible for everything the MacGregors did.

Reportedly, he didn't have much luck controlling them, either, and by now he may have been tired of the whole mess. Only a few years after the Act of General Ban was enacted, he went back to the Crown to get permission to suppress the "wicked" MacGregors and various other "broken" men of the Highlands. Perhaps not entirely coincidentally, he was also starting to be in need of a little influx of cash at this particular point in time, given some things he'd been doing over in Ireland that were starting to become a little worrisome, messy, and expensive and would eventually tie his fortunes to the Nine Years' War in Ireland.

But back to his MacGregor problems.

Years after the Act of General Ban, the Colquhouns were complaining bitterly about the MacGregors to anyone else who would listen, and they were not only complaining to

Argyll, by now they were complaining a bit *about* Argyll for failing to comply with the Act and control the MacGregor "menace."

Not coincidentally, in the aftermath of what happened after the Battle of Fruin, Argyll featured heavily.

There was also more than a hint of nefarious doings.

So. Now we need to return to the Colquhoun version of what happened to the two men who were killed over a sheep. In this version, the circumstances were vastly different.

According to the Colquhouns, it wasn't about hospitality, and it wasn't two MacGregor men who were killed.

Instead, it was two *Colquhoun* men who were murdered by MacGregors in yet another MacGregor raid. And in place of a single sheep, black or otherwise, the MacGregors reportedly rode away with 300 Colquhoun cows, 100 horses, 400 sheep, and 400 goats.

Perhaps if it involved a smaller number of animals, this version of the story might be more believable. Trying to herd that many animals—of vastly different sizes and temperaments—through the Highland passes to MacGregor land would have been very difficult, though, and would have required a lot of manpower at any time of year. In December, it would have been a formidable task requiring much preparation, and the Colquhoun men would have fought hard to prevent the loss of that many animals. Such a loss would have represented tremendous hardship in the coming winter.

So let's take this with a grain of salt.

Meanwhile, long and—potentially dubious—story short, since the Earl of Argyll was now responsible for the behavior of the MacGregors, the Colquhouns went to him with their new complaint. Argyll counseled them to take the bloody shirts of the two murdered men straight to King James VI, the son of Mary Queen of Scots. Which they did.

King James duly gave the Colquhouns the right to bear arms against the MacGregors and pursue them with impunity. In other words, a hunting license and it was MacGregor season.

What happened next, though, isn't entirely clear. Because the Colquhouns did not go hunting.

Either they sat back to wait for better weather, or maybe they somehow incited what happened next. Whichever the case, the subsequent round of action didn't occur on MacGregor land with Colquhouns in pursuit.

It occurred when the MacGregors returned to Glen Fruin in force.

And after that, for a while, the stories all agree.

Having mustered clansmen and allies, fewer than 400 MacGregors marched to Glen Fruin in early February. But the Colquhouns had been warned, and they had already gathered at least twice as many fighters, including 300 horsemen and 500 additional men on foot.

The Colquhouns were so certain of their victory that they brought along some young students from the Collegiate School of Dumbarton to watch and learn how they were going to deal with those who troubled them.

Unfortunately for the students—and the Colquhouns— the battle didn't go as expected. The MacGregors fought both intelligently and fiercely, and they left so many Colquhouns dead that the Colquhoun survivors—and the Earl of Argyll—reported the battle to King James as a massacre, laying the "murder" of 140 Colquhoun men squarely on the MacGregors.

Once again, King James was persuaded to take their side.

Interestingly, some accounts say that the MacGregors also killed the young men from the college, but oddly, this wasn't in the official complaint made to James against them.

Instead, it was the massacre of the eighteen MacLaren men in the Balquhidder glen way back in 1558 that was added to the charges of butchering Colquhoun men at the Battle of Glen Fruin. Yes, that's forty-five years after the fact, in case you're keeping track.

By this time, King James felt he'd had quite enough of the MacGregors, thank you very much. Not only were they still Catholics, which in the mind of many was bad enough, but according to the reports, they were primarily charged with just being awful people.

On February 24, 1603, James and his Privy Council passed the Proscriptive Acts of the Clan MacGregor, which ordered that the "unhappie and detestable" MacGregor "race" should be "extirpat and ruttit out, and never suffered to have rest or remaining within this countrey hierafter." The Acts abolished even the use of the MacGregor name on pain of death, and made it legal to hunt MacGregors by any means.

Eventually, Alastair MacGregor of Glen Strae and his men, charged with the murder of the 140 Colquhoun men for the Battle of Fruin, were caught. Alastair negotiated safe passage out of the country to England with the Earl of Argyll—who was, remember, a close relative, since Alastair was the son of the Marion Campbell who had married Gregor MacGregor. But Argyll then promptly turned Alastair and eleven of his chieftains over to the Scottish authorities for execution.

The men were hanged on a single cross, and Alastair—after some judicious torture—was hanged a head's height above them as their chief.

But there's even a further whiff of Campbell treachery.

Alastair, in his last confession, blamed the Campbells for having instigated the raid on the Colquhouns in a bid to enrich themselves. And remembering the subordinate and over-a-barrel position in which Alastair had found himself with Black Duncan, this isn't implausible from a practical perspective.

From a spiritual perspective, it makes still more sense. As a Catholic, it would have been pointless for Alastair to make a false confession, since anything but a full and truthful one would not have resulted in absolution. Either Alastair was telling the truth, or he was fully prepared to forgo salvation to implicate the Campbells falsely.

It's an interesting question.

Once Alastair was gone, with no land of their own for sanctuary and even their name forbidden to them, the

MacGregor clan retreated to remote places in the Highlands and came to be known as the Children of the Mist. MacGregor women were stripped, branded, and whipped through the streets, and MacGregor men, regardless of the name they used, could not carry so much as a pointed knife. They could be robbed or killed with impunity, and the killing of a MacGregor was not merely *not* a crime, it was to be encouraged. The killer sometimes even earned a reward.

Technically, no child could be baptized a MacGregor, and clerks and notaries were prohibited from subscribing bond or other securities to anyone who bore the MacGregor name, which made it impossible for them to transfer property or conduct business. What land they held, they had to hold by the sword, and—without property titles—this made them even more vulnerable to their powerful neighbors.

In 1661, Charles II briefly rewarded the clan by lifting the Proscription Acts in exchange for the loyalty of the MacGregors in fighting with James Graham, the Duke of Montrose, on the side of the Scottish Royalists in support of his father, Charles I. (The Campbells fought on the opposite, pro-Covenanter, side.) But William of Orange renewed the Acts again in 1693. The MacGregors then fought on the side of the Jacobites in the Risings of 1715 and 1745, and it wasn't until 1774 that the Acts were permanently repealed.

The Children of the Mist

"The moon's on the lake, and the mist's on the brae,
And the Clan has a name that is nameless by day."

SIR WALTER SCOTT
"MACGREGORS GATHERING"

R OB ROY, OR ROBERT THE RED, was the third son of the MacGregor chief, Donald Gregor of Glengyle. His mother was Margaret Campbell, a cousin of John Iain Campbell, the eleventh Laird of Glenorchy (which the Campbells had taken from the MacGregors a few centuries earlier). John Iain later became the Earl of Breadalbane and eventually the second Duke of Argyll. All this is a bit ironic, considering the treacherous role the Campbells of Glenorchy and the Earl of Argyll had played earlier in getting the MacGregors outlawed and their name proscribed.

But outlawed or not, the MacGregors did still have allies. This was true all the way through the harsh history of

Scotland—and it continued through the Jacobite Risings. Neighbors, friendships, family—these all suffered due to politics, but loyalties often supersede law and allegiance to a king or lord or government. Some of this had to do with the women, who managed to maintain contact and form the core of steel that bound everyone together.

Despite the prohibitions on the MacGregor, and Gregor, names, Rob Roy was baptized Robert MacGregor, but he used his mother's Campbell name for much of his life. And like his wild red hair, his exploits were very colorful.

Although he was a Protestant himself, Rob first came to prominence as he rallied his father's clansmen in support of the deposed King James. At the time of the Battle of Killicrankie, he was just eighteen.

Killicrankie, the decisive military engagement of the earliest of the Scottish Jacobite "Risings," was hard and bloody, and the Jacobite leader Viscount "Bonnie" Dundee, John Graham, was killed there in the fight against the forces of William of Orange. (More about Bonnie Dundee later.) With his death and the Jacobite defeat, Rob Roy's father was then imprisoned for two years for treason, during which time he lost both his health and his wife, who had died in his absence.

Along with his brothers, Rob Roy was left to manage the family business, raising cattle with a little raiding on the side, and he became known for his shrewd mind and was respected as a businessman, gradually increasing the family holdings. He married happily and had four sons. By all accounts, he was doing well despite all the hardships imposed on the MacGregor clan.

During this time, he often did business with the Duke of Montrose, for whom he made quite a bit of money. (Quite possibly a cut of the proceeds from cattle raiding and his "blackmailing" racket in addition to the more legitimate trade.)

Having known Montrose relatively well for ten years, then, when Rob needed money to expand his cattle business, he turned to Montrose for a loan of £1,000 pounds, which at the time was an enormous fortune. He entrusted the money to an employee to deliver, but when the man was robbed—possibly by an agent of Montrose's—the duke saw a chance and had Rob branded as an outlaw for embezzlement and seized Rob's land and cattle for himself.

Rob next turned to his mother's cousin for help. The new Duke of Argyll, a political enemy of Montrose, allowed Rob to rent property on his own land, from where Rob (with the Duke's at least tacit blessing) exacted revenge against Montrose for his greed and betrayal through a series of raids and constant harassment.

Montrose, naturally, didn't take this quietly, and his pursuit of Rob and his family was both ruthless and relentless. For Rob, the situation was further complicated by the fact that the Campbells and MacGregors found themselves on opposing sides in a wider war.

Rob rallied again to the Jacobite cause in 1715, and that, in the end, only made all of his problems worse. To understand why, it's necessary to take a brief detour through the history of Ireland, Scotland, and England leading up to the Jacobite uprisings that were meant to restore the crown of the royal house of Stuart.

Henry Needs A Divorce

*"O, how wretched
Is that poor man that hangs on princes' favours!"*

WILLIAM SHAKESPEARE
HENRY VIII

NOW BUCKLE YOUR SEATBELTS. This gets a little convoluted. But it's also interesting, because in many ways, it has parallels to what is going on in the world today.

The Jacobite period, and the few hundred years leading up to it, were incredibly hard on the people who had to live in Ireland, Scotland, and England (including Wales and Cornwall). There was turmoil, hardship, persecution, and outright genocide in some cases, along with alliances that shifted at lighting speed. Homes that had been in people's families for hundreds of years were stripped away; men, women, and children were torn from their beds; and young and old, male and female alike, were often murdered in horrible and brutal ways. And what people were taught to believe about the God who was the foundation for their faith and how they worshiped and lived their lives was rocked to the core.

From a fiction perspective, I love this period of history. Along with conflict, it created amazing heroes and heroines—and villains—aplenty, people with larger-than-life personalities who were willing to fight to defend their families and lay down their lives for what they believed. And in my books, I love to show how all these historical wars have created some of the problems my characters face in the present, modern world.

The aftermath of the events I'm about to go over are still being felt in many ways. In the United States, we owe our belief in freedom of religion to people fleeing many of these struggles. The misogyny currently being addressed in the #MeToo and #TimesUp movements arguably has some foundation in how the Puritan men who settled the colonies saw women. As we tackle modern issues of diversity, there are echoes back to how the Irish were treated when they first arrived in New York and Boston, among other places, to escape the persecution and starvation into which the English had pushed them in Ireland. Yet ironically, it was sometimes

Scots and other Irish who had committed the atrocities. As we face a global population explosion, we can look back to England between 1520 and 1630, when the population doubled and they dealt with the problem of unemployment and "idleness" by shipping people off to other countries. The system of "plantation"—the seeding of loyal English subjects into a territory and then supplying them with cheap, forced labor—first through indentured servitude and then through slavery—became the cornerstone of oppression for centuries. And some of those conflicts may well return to the forefront in the British Isles, given the nature of Brexit— Britain's historic vote to separate from the European Union. Questions about the border between Ireland, an EU member, and Northern Ireland, part of Great Britain, as well as some differences in Brexit support in Scotland versus England, could conceivably reignite struggles set in motion by Henry VIII and his children.

Like I said, buckle your seatbelts . . .

We're about to head onto the turbulent road leading to the Jacobite Risings.

Once upon a time, it all began when Henry Tudor decided he needed a divorce. Oh, and the invention of the printing press.

Seriously.

At the time, there was no precedent in modern—for the time—English history that allowed the Crown to pass to anyone but a male heir, and Henry didn't want to push his luck. England had just emerged from the bloody War of the Roses, a series of civil wars between the supporters of the Lancaster and York branches of the ruling Plantagenet family, which had, in turn, been partly the result of a weak Lancaster king (Henry VI), the aftermath of the Hundred Years' War, and various feudal policies. The people of England were basically sick of fighting each other, so Henry desperately needed a male heir.

Now Henry, as a man, was a mass of contradictions. He was the second son—and third child—of Henry VII, but his brother Arthur died suddenly when Henry was only ten. His father was distraught. The family had already lost three other children who hadn't survived infancy, and the loss of his heir was an enormous blow to the royal couple, who seemed to have a truly happy marriage. With Arthur gone and only one son left, the king showered all his affection and hope onto young Henry, along with the weight of responsibility, in turns indulging him dangerously and then reining him in with austere measures. Where Henry had begun to be brought up studying theology with the ultimate aim of becoming a priest, now he was suddenly destined to be the king.

Henry was a handsome boy with a quick intelligence and an insatiable eagerness for learning. He had a sharp eye for politics and events, not only in England but all through Europe, and he prided himself in knowing what was going on. He also had an artistic side, writing music as well as playing it. And he excelled at athletic pursuits, archery, riding, tennis, and jousting. Had he been brought up more reasonably, he might have been an entirely different man. But by the time he inherited the throne at the age of eighteen, he was a mass of contradictions—a romantic in outlook who saw himself as the hero of some grand story, a savior of his people, a knight in shining armor, but also a shrewd and brutal pragmatist on the political stage who demanded his own way and was clever enough to find creative new legal ways to get it. In later years, he grew increasingly egotistical, unreasonable, vain—also fat and depressed about his appearance and loss of youth. Desperate to raise England to be the equal or better of any nation on earth, he engaged in a series of wars and campaigns, and he needed a dynasty to maintain his vision, a son to whom he could pass the torch.

Catherine (sometimes Katharine) of Aragon, his first

wife, was actually his brother Arthur's widow. The marriage of Catherine's father—the king of Sicily and Aragon—and her mother—the queen of Castile—had created the foundation of modern Spain, so at the time of Arthur's death, the alliance had been seen as critical. So much so that Henry's father had gone to the pope to get a special dispensation for Henry to marry Catherine. He'd also contemplated marrying her himself. Neither of those things happened before his death, but on taking the throne, Henry had decided to give it a go. But in twenty years, despite giving birth to many children, Catherine hadn't managed to give him a surviving son, only a daughter who would eventually become Queen Mary. And she didn't seem likely to have much more success in the future. Also, by this time, Henry was infatuated with Anne Boleyn, so—maybe—by then he'd stopped trying *all* that hard. Anyway, Henry asked the pope to sign off on an annulment of the marriage based on a little bit of tricky logic, which basically said that since Catherine had been his brother's widow, the marriage hadn't been strictly legal to begin with, so, therefore, it had never happened. But the pope, knowing this was kind of a no-win situation since he didn't want to upset Catherine's Spanish parents and Spain was an increasingly powerful Catholic force, decided not to get around to answering Henry's request anytime soon.

So what did Henry do? Well, he wasn't terribly patient, and since Anne refused to become his mistress, he decided he *had* to marry her. He appointed a new Archbishop of Canterbury, who duly annulled Henry's marriage as he requested, and then secretly married him to Anne in 1532. The pope wasn't thrilled, and he excommunicated both Henry and the Archbishop.

Now here's where Henry got clever. Being head of the English branch of the Catholic Church when you were no longer technically a Catholic was a little thorny. So, he decided to start his own religion, one where he, instead of the pope, got to be in charge of the church. That way, he wouldn't ever have to worry about the pesky pope having more power than he did.

This may all sound a little far-fetched now, but I was lucky enough to get to see the actual appeal that Henry sent to the Vatican, along with the wax seals of eighty-odd English bishops, cardinals, and lords, at a display of the secret Vatican archives at the Capitoline museum in 2012. This was one of many documents that when seen altogether reveal the gradual rise of papacy, through a series of bulls and power grabs, that—at least from the perspective of monarchs like Henry—eroded what had previously been the autonomy of nations, which Henry and others believed had been granted to their sovereigns directly by God—working through, naturally, the instrument of a large and brutal army in most cases. To Henry, therefore, getting Parliament to help him set himself up as the head of the Church of England via the First Act of Supremacy in 1534 made perfect sense. He was able to sell the idea in England, too, partly because he was very good at politics, but also because—ironically— he had a track record of being the "Defender of the Faith"— a title the pope had given him back in 1521 for his work in attacking Martin Luther's ideas on flaws in the Catholic religion.

Naturally, not everyone in England and Ireland agreed with all of this. (Scotland was a separate country at this point, ruled by Henry's nephew, James V.) Henry came down swiftly on people who opposed him—and he was pretty fond of executing people for treason, actually—but, at least at first, he didn't make too many other changes to the way people worshiped or in what they were supposed to believe. And whatever he asked of others, he personally stuck very close to most of the Catholic ideas of faith and worship until the end of his life.

Back, however, to the divorce. The negotiations all took a while, but in 1534, Henry finally got his wish. After twenty-four years of marriage, Catherine of Aragon was out, and Henry got to marry Anne Boleyn. Officially. Unofficially, he'd already married her in secret in 1532, well before the annulment of his marriage to Catherine had been approved by the new Church of England.

Patience wasn't Henry's strong suit.

Oh, and the pope did weigh in eventually—well after the fact—to say that Henry's marriage to Anne wasn't valid by a long shot.

Anne, meanwhile, didn't last long, either. Although she gave birth to his daughter Elizabeth, who would later become Queen Elizabeth I, three months after being crowned as queen of England, but she didn't give him a male heir fast enough. And now he had a new infatuation. Having finally bedded Anne, he'd grown tired of her, and he'd set his sights on marrying Jane Seymour. Since he'd already gone through the long, painful annulment thing once, he took a shortcut this time and had Anne accused of treason. She was beheaded a month later, so really, for Henry, this was much more convenient.

Okay, so now Henry'd had two wives and two daughters who, thanks to his own bed-hopping and creativity, were both technically illegitimate. And he still had no son. Plus all those reasons why he really needed to bring some stability to the line of succession hadn't magically gone away.

And remember Martin Luther? The guy who had written a long list of why the Catholic Church wasn't such a good idea?

There was a new player on the field as well. John Calvin founded the Reformed Church in Geneva in 1536, and his ideas were spreading. Thanks to the invention of the printing press a while back, information and *ideas* could be transmitted far more easily and books were no longer the exclusive playgrounds of the rich and the Catholic Church, and the first decades of Henry's life were at the height of the Renaissance, a time of unprecedented intellectual debate and literacy. With the printing press and word of mouth, both Luther's as well as Calvin's ideas gained traction in Europe and began new forms of religion. Together with later reforms in the Church of England, this set the foundation for the three major branches of Protestantism.

Confused about the differences between Catholics and Protestants? So were most people.

Bear in mind, the vast majority of folks caught up in all of this, both Catholic and Protestant, didn't really care about the politics of any of it. They were simply trying to survive in a very harsh world, feed their families, and live their lives in peace, being good and faithful in the best way they could. Much like today, what they believed was governed by what their clerics, parents, teachers, and neighbors believed, or what they were forced to believe because the people in charge of them didn't give them any choice. But having even the appearance of having a choice, of being able to be informed and to make decisions on their own, was exceedingly seductive. And the idea of getting rid of corruption that had kept them oppressed? What was not to like?

Here's a very quick and dirty cheat sheet, which admittedly leaves out a lot of important nuance on all sides:

- Catholics think the pope has full power over the church. Protestants don't agree.

- Catholics believe "good works" can influence one's salvation, while Protestants believe their standing with God derives purely from their faith. For

Catholics, this means that good deeds, including prayers and forgiveness, can mitigate past wrongs.

- Catholics believe both the traditions of the church and the Bible provide authority in matters of faith, but Protestants acknowledge authority from the Bible only. Catholic services contain many complex traditions and symbols of worship that take time to learn and navigate, while Protestant worship tends to be simpler and more straightforward, and, therefore, accessible to more people.

- Catholics consider that, in the rite of Holy Communion, the bread and wine is transubstantiated into the blood of Jesus Christ. Protestants consider the bread and wine representations of the body and blood of Christ.

- Catholics also pray to Mary as the "Mother of God" and to other saints to intercede with her Son on their behalf. In the early history of the church, some of these saints helped unify and consolidate other religions and cultures, with Catholic saints taking on some of the characteristics and feast days of earlier deities. Protestants recognize Mary as the mother of Christ, but they don't usually pray to her.

- Catholic ecclesiastical structure is hierarchical and regimented, and services are centered on ritual, rites, liturgy, and symbolism with focus on the Holy Communion and an underlying note of awe and mystery. Protestant Church structure is less ordered, and church services are primarily focused on the sermon.

- In Catholicism, only men can be priests and they must remain celibate. Traditionally, this came about partly to preserve wealth for the church, because married priests would naturally have wanted to provide for their children, whereas those without heirs left everything to the church—and many priests came from wealthy families. In various modern Protestant Churches, women can become clerics and hold positions of power, and clerics can marry and bear children.

At first glance, these differences don't seem nearly vast enough to account for a fraction of the deaths and tragedy that came about in the course of the Protestant Reformation and the push back from the Catholic establishment. Or the reversal later. Or the reversal after that.

In practice, though, remember that the Reformation was

about far more, and its ideas were attractive to people whose lives were painfully hard. While the core beliefs of Catholicism were, at the beginning of Reformation, the same as they had ever been and were still meant to provide solace and relief for rich and poor alike, the fifteenth-century ecclesiastical establishment had grown deeply corrupt. Churches were visibly full of gold and jewels and the trappings of wealth, clergy lived very well indeed, and many high church officials lived like kings. To gain and keep that wealth, the church played politics. Brutally.

Wealth, overall, was (and is) hard to get and keep if you were strictly playing "fair" or being "good" or "godly." This went for the aristocrats of Europe as well as for the members of the church establishment. But because the Catholic faith allowed for the idea of penance to forgive past sins, unscrupulous people could get away with a lot and be "forgiven." It became commonplace to trade in penance. Need a new cathedral? Tell the citizens they can get *future* sins forgiven by donating to the church. After which, those who have donated the most can, in practice, go out and exploit the peasants with impunity. Want to control the masses? Keep everything about your religion shrouded in secrecy, written in a language that only the clerics and nobility can understand, much less read, and then tell the peasants only what you want them to hear. Whether this was or wasn't the intention originally, in the corrupt environment of the sixteenth century, this was how many viewed the Catholic Church establishment.

In other words, the Protestant Reformation wasn't merely about religion. It was about equality and freedom from social control. It was about *access*.

Of course, not every Catholic was then or ever had been "bad." And just as there were many Catholics who were truly devout, there were many among the new Protestant "reformers" who were simply grasping at opportunities to seize power and improve their own lives. Even where it came to these people, though, that didn't necessarily mean they didn't care about the lives of the people to whom they were preaching. Just as motivation was mixed and varied among Catholics, it was complicated among Protestants, too. Humans are and always have been able to find ways to serve their own interests and make themselves believe they are right and justified. In fact, quite often, the more one has to gain for oneself in the course of serving a "greater" cause— whether that is peace of mind, position and fame, or material wealth—the more zealous one becomes about the cause itself. And the louder and more brutally one tends to vilify others on the opposing side.

The Reformation, and the Counter-Reformation, sparked wars and persecutions all over Europe. They encouraged social reform, new depths of thinking about faith, new standards of behavior. They fostered new atrocities. At every step, wealth changed hands. Power waxed and waned.

And it was too often the ordinary people, the powerless people, who suffered or were vilified disproportionately.

In England, at the beginning, change came with deceptive ease. Getting people to give up their religion just because Henry the VIII needed a divorce wasn't going to fly with the masses, for example, so he had to sell it a different way.

Since his foundation of the Church of England coincided with the Protestant movement in Europe, and the arrival of Protestantism in England, Scotland, and to a lesser degree, Ireland, Henry took a few of the ideas of Martin Luther and John Calvin and used them to justify his actions. On the other hand, he also dissolved the monasteries and grabbed their wealth.

He began distributing Bibles. (But more about that later

when we return to Scotland.)

Meanwhile, with Jane Seymour, his third wife, Henry had finally produced a legitimate male heir, who eventually became King Edward VI, and Henry managed to live nine years after that. This period saw him through a couple more wars, the whole Bible-distribution thing, and some other problems, but Edward was still very young when his father died and he inherited the throne.

With his father's large personality and grandiose spending looming over him, Edward had emerged to be more like his grandfather—frugal and reserved to the point of stoicism, but also intelligent and charming. But he'd been raised staunchly Protestant, with authoritatively Calvinist overtones. And at nine, he was young. Very young. Also, his regents—the men who de facto governed in his name, first the Duke of Somerset and then the Duke of Northumberland—were eager to seize as much power as they could for themselves.

That all didn't necessarily go well, especially in Scotland where during Edward's regency, British forces were forced to withdraw. Riots and rebellion brewed all over the place. Things were changing too fast, which always makes people edgy and belligerent. Then, too, there was a power vacuum, and there were a lot of people willing to take advantage of all of that.

Poor Edward was only fifteen when it became clear he was dying of tuberculosis. He didn't have any heirs, so the question of succession now came back in play. Given the whole propensity the country had demonstrated in the past few hundred years of going to war over who was in charge, that didn't bode well for England.

With Edward's young age and failing health, it's not entirely clear how much of what happened next was his own idea and how much was down to the influence of the Duke of Northumberland, but Edward made it very clear he didn't want to see a Catholic on the throne.

Now, though, do you remember how, in the course of his religious and matrimonial scheming, Henry VIII, Edward's father, had somehow managed to have both his daughters, Mary and Elizabeth, made arguably illegitimate? To restore them to the line of succession, he'd had to jump through some more legal hoops. The Third Succession Act of 1544 gave them each, in turn, the right to rule should anything happen to Edward. But—and it's a big *but*—it also opened the door for the throne to pass to the children of Henry's sister, Mary, if his own children died without heirs of their own.

It was this wedge in the door that was exploited by Edward and Northumberland in trying to keep Edward's Catholic half-sister, Mary, from the throne. Instead of passing the throne to either her or his other half-sister Elizabeth, Edward named his aunt Mary Tudor's seventeen-year-old—and equally staunchly Protestant—grand-daughter, Jane Grey, as his heir and married her to Northumberland's son, Lord Guildford Dudley. Poor Lady Jane Grey, as she is known, was queen for only nine days after Edward's death, from July 10 to July 19, 1553. That's how long it took for Edward's sister Mary to win her crown and sweep in on a tide of triumph and popular rejoicing to become England's first queen regnant—a monarch in her own right. She had both Jane and her husband executed in 1554.

Now, as I've said before, Mary was Catholic, but she'd been able to rally popular support and an army faster than the Duke of Northumberland, despite all his conniving. The wave of popular support for her was enormous. So far so good. All was well, right?

Not so fast.

Mary was a deeply troubled woman. Doted on in her early childhood by her father, Henry VIII, she had been a sweet, good-natured child. But Anne Boleyn was an ambitious woman, determined to sit on the throne instead of Catherine—and determined also to see her own daughter, Elizabeth, seated there. In short order, poor Mary went from being Henry's pampered princess, and the heir to his crown, to being the "illegitimate" child, an embarrassment and an impediment that stood in the way of Anne Boleyn's machinations. But both Catherine of Aragon and Mary herself stubbornly opposed Henry's demands, refusing to admit that Mary was anything but the legitimate heir to Henry's throne—and refusing to make a public declaration supporting that Henry was the head of the church.

To get his way on both counts, Henry resorted to cruelty. He had Mary locked up. He denied her food. He denied her warm clothing. (No, he wasn't a nice man, in case you hadn't picked up on this earlier.) A whisper campaign was started, and deliberately leaked to Mary, that Anne Boleyn was planning on poisoning Mary, torturing her, and/or having her raped. Stripped not only of her previously luxurious and pampered life but of virtually all security and affection, Mary had nothing but her faith to sustain her through all this. And since she'd been raised devoutly Catholic by her Spanish mother, this was a Catholic faith. She became increasingly devout. And she learned to distrust the duplicitous English.

Still, she held out. It was only after Anne Boleyn herself had been executed, her own mother had died, and Henry had married Jane Seymour that Mary finally gave in, perhaps out of sheer exhaustion. The document she signed at Henry's insistence not only admitted that her parents' marriage had been against the law and she herself was, therefore, illegitimate, it confirmed that Henry VIII was the Supreme Head in Earth under Christ of the Church of England.

She felt like a traitor to her faith from the moment she affixed her signature to that paper. And she had felt guilty about it every day since. By the time she took the throne, Mary was determined to make what she saw as reparations to her church and faith.

On seizing power, she started rolling back the Protestant reforms that first Henry, and then Edward and his regents, had put in place. Power shifted again, real people were affected, and many objected. Mary ruled for only five years, but in that time, she had nearly 300 Protestants and religious dissenters burned alive at the stake. She came to be known as "Bloody Mary."

Desperate to produce a Catholic heir, and having come through Henry's matrimonial machinations deeply scarred, Mary suffered through the very public humiliation of a "false pregnancy." Mentally, she was so convinced that she was pregnant that her body exhibited all the outward signs. For nine months, the country watched her preparing to give birth, and then her confinement approached. All the baby clothes were ready. The country waited. Mary waited. And nothing happened. The doctors decided the dates must have been wrong, but another month passed, and another, and the outward signs gradually receded. The pregnancy was never mentioned. But obviously, Mary wasn't exactly stable after that.

And then came Elizabeth, Mary's half-sister. Another Protestant.

Do you feel like you're at a ping-pong match? Imagine how the people of England and Ireland must have felt . . .

Elizabeth was both her father's daughter and her mother's. Which is to say that she was intelligent, well educated, and capable of great charm when she wanted to get her way, but she was also ruthless, shrewd, and deeply, skillfully conniving. As a child, she was set up in the most brutal way to replace her sister Mary, and was then later, in turn, replaced by Edward—both in her father's affections and in the succession to the throne. Her mother was beheaded for treason, and she herself was declared illegitimate. Then, by the time Elizabeth was ten years old, four more wives had passed through her father's bed. Edward's mother had died twelve days after giving birth to the boy, then Henry had his marriage to Anne of Cleves annulled, and finally he had Catherine Howard beheaded. Perhaps fortunately for Catherine Parr, Henry died before he could figure out he wanted to be rid of her as well.

Henry left a country that was deeply impoverished by a long series of wars and his own excesses, deeply divided on religious grounds and on the question of succession. He did manage to bring Wales to heel under the English Crown, and he also gave himself a promotion from Henry, Lord of Ireland to Henry, *King* of Ireland. But not only were his steps to annul his marriage to Catherine of Aragon not valid in the eyes of any good Catholic, but he himself had affirmed Elizabeth's own illegitimacy and proclaimed it for years. A single signature from Henry on the Acts of Succession wasn't able to sweep all that away.

Horse, barn, door.

In the view of many English subjects, and especially in

the minds of European Catholic monarchs, Elizabeth didn't really have the right to be queen. And for countries like Spain and France, especially, an illegitimate queen on the English throne was a sign of weakness—and an opportunity.

Elizabeth had seen enough queens beheaded to understand perfectly the position that she was in. If her own mother's death hadn't drummed this home, the fact that her sister Mary had had her locked up in the Tower of London (granted, yes, it was a palace, but it was also clearly a prison) on taking the throne, had brought the danger home in deeply terrifying terms. Elizabeth was so afraid that she refused to go into the Tower at first, which led to a stalemate because she was still royal and couldn't be dragged in. Eventually, cold and hunger forced her inside, and for the five years of Mary's reign, she lived in fear.

So, on taking the throne herself, Elizabeth was determined that she was going to be invulnerable.

Being clever as well as intelligent, she embarked on one of the greatest public relations campaigns in all of history, cultivating a glittering image that projected power, glamour, and English patriotism. She cultivated poets, playwrights, and pamphleteers, and artists who helped her spread this image far and wide. And through the long years of her reign, she successfully played countries and courtiers alike against each other with consummate skill, using everything from flirtation, the promise of marriage, political alliances, favor, and even the general perceptions most people had of women to mask her true intentions and intelligence.

Among Catholics, there was not a little objection to going back to a Protestant monarch at first, not least because they feared yet another round of retaliation and persecution. This was a real fear, chiefly in Ireland, where many people also just wanted to be Irish instead of being second-class citizens of England.

Beyond the Pale

*"To be Irish is to know that in the end
the world will break your heart."*

DANIEL PATRICK MOYNIHAN

SEPARATE FROM ENGLAND, THE Irish had never really been an undisputedly united country. As in Wales, which Henry VIII had successfully and finally annexed in 1536, there were too many different princes and chiefs who were fighting for supremacy in the wake of the Norman invasion of Ireland, which had begun in 1169 but never really managed to take firm control outside of small pockets like Dublin and Galway. The small section of English control that was centered on Dublin and extended south along the coast was called the Pale—which stemmed from the practice (that had begun with Catharine the Great and the Jews of Russia) of picketing or fencing off areas beyond which it wasn't safe or acceptable for civilized people to live or go.

The idea of something being "beyond the Pale"—which you might see in Regency novels—was often used when someone or something broke with "civil" or "acceptable" behavior. That right there tells you a lot about how the English viewed the rest of Ireland. In Galway, where the Norman lord had become too "Gaelic" for the English families within the city, the merchants walled themselves off and stated that "NEITHER O' NOR MAC SHALL STRUTTE NOR SWAGGER THROUGH THE STREETS OF GALWAY" without permission.

Having the Norman-Irish lords go "native" had become a bit of a problem for the English after the Norman Conquest in Ireland. Without much governmental influence after the initial "conquest," the Norman settlers in the Pale and elsewhere made alliances with neighboring Irish chiefs and princes who came and went as the chiefs disagreed with them and warred amongst themselves. During the Hundred Years' War and the War of the Roses, the English were too busy killing each other to worry much about the Irish, so the size of the Pale gradually shrank to the most defensible areas in the fertile lowlands and outside the Pale the Norman lords grew increasingly Gaelicized. Basically, they went native.

Meanwhile, English monarchs had fallen into the habit

of giving Irish land and titles willy-nilly to Englishmen. (They were good at this—they did the same in Wales, Cornwall, and Scotland.) Then, too, there was the way the native Irish were treated. The Parliament of Ireland, set up in the thirteenth century based on the English pattern, allowed only the "English of Ireland" to be represented, but the Parliament's decisions, mostly relating to taxation and "peacekeeping," were chiefly applied to Irish citizens, who had no say in the matter. Entire companies of Crown soldiers, along with their wives, children, servants, and friends, would head to where crops were being harvested, force the farmers and landowners to feed them, then take what they wanted and often spoil or burn the rest. Rape and murder often went along with this for good measure. In place of Irish Gaelic, English had become the official language.

The native Irish, naturally, didn't appreciate this, and they strenuously objected. And when some of the "English-Irish" families had to go off to England to fight in the various wars, the Irish took advantage of the situation and rose up to take back what they viewed as rightfully theirs.

But with the end of the War of the Roses, the English-Irish families came back, and having fought on opposing sides, they still had scores to settle in addition to trying to reclaim the properties the Irish had taken back. More unrest ensued, which Henry VIII tried to subdue by upgrading his title to King of England and Ireland—we've already seen that he liked taking power. He also paved the way for this with a very cheap, and somewhat sneaky, slight of hand called "surrender and regrant," which basically gave the Gaelic-Irish and English-Irish lords incentives to "give" their land to the English Crown and immediately get it "granted" back to them at nominal annual rent with perks like seats in the Irish Parliament, assorted protections, and no armed conflict. The sneaky part? Well, they had to agree to give up that pesky Catholicism and accept English Salic law in place of their native Gaelic Brehon law. Oh, and also accept that future inheritance of property would be through primogeniture instead of through the Gaelic custom of elected tanistry to decide the chief of a clan. And here's the really sneaky part. A number of the Gaelic chiefs who submitted to surrender and regrant weren't the elected *tánaiste,* or chosen heir, of their clans—and the lands they surrendered weren't actually theirs to begin with. This had the added bonus, from Henry's point of view, of keeping those clans fighting within themselves instead of organizing to fight the changes he was imposing.

Meanwhile, the Irish Parliament had enacted increasingly tougher restrictions on the Gaelic Irish. From 1465, Irish living within the Pale had to dress and groom themselves like the English, had to take English surnames based on a color, their place of residence, or their occupation, and were limited how and with whom they could trade. The new restrictions allowed for any "thief"—defined not only as someone who had actually stolen something, but also as anyone who was caught *going* somewhere without an accompanying Englishman—to be summarily decapitated. Oh, and by the way, if any loyal citizen brought the head of such a "thief" to the nearest town, the major was authorized to pay them a nice reward.

Hmm. No incentive there for abuse.

Okay, so by this time, the Irish were not loving English occupation so much.

The next phase, under Queen Elizabeth, was the Nine Years' War in Ireland, which was also known as Tyrone's Rebellion.

The Tragic Queen

*"I fear John Knox's prayers more
Than an army of ten thousand men."*

MARY QUEEN OF SCOTS

IRELAND WASN'T SOMETHING ELIZABETH wanted to deal with. She had enough problems at home and in Scotland, and both France and Spain were doing their best at various power grabs. But there was the rub, so to speak, if she left a power vacuum in either Ireland or Scotland, she was afraid that she'd end up with the French or Spanish literally at her doorstep, and in a much stronger position for invasion. While dealing with her Scottish problems, therefore, she fired off instructions designed to tame Ireland once and for all, making it more thoroughly "English" with a series of harsh reforms.

Her efforts in Ireland were soon to have serious consequences, but while those play out in the background, we need to go back to Scotland, which has been ruled by Stewarts (now Stuarts) since way, way back in the fourteenth century when Robert the Bruce's daughter married Walter Steward, the sixth High Steward of Scotland.

And remember those neatly tricky hoops that Henry jumped through to deal with his various marriages? The ones that made both Mary and Elizabeth illegitimate?

Yes, we're back to that. Again.

Because . . .

If one was Catholic and didn't want a Protestant queen, or if one believed that an illegitimate daughter of the king shouldn't be the monarch, or if one didn't want an English monarch at all when the English didn't tend, historically, to treat one's country very well, or if one happened to be French or Irish or Scottish and loved one's own country, one might have some incentive to support someone other than Queen Elizabeth I as the true and rightful ruler.

Also, Henry (along with his son Edward and the Duke of Northumberland) had already opened the door that allowed a hint of a claim from Mary Tudor's offspring to claim the throne of England.

This was compounded by Elizabeth's failure to marry and produce an heir of her own.

In her defense, Elizabeth had many really good reasons for choosing to stay single. Initially, marriage could have taken away some of her bargaining power, and choosing one contender might have lost her more than she stood to gain from any prospective match. Even more importantly, it would have cost her power that she wanted—and felt she deserved—for herself. At that time, any man she married would have become the de facto king—not a consort. That would have placed him in a more powerful position than Elizabeth, and it would have brought foreign influence and interests to England, something that neither Elizabeth nor her subjects wanted.

And Elizabeth wasn't about to put herself into any position of weakness. Given her father's matrimonial contortions, she'd seen and lived through the very emotional and lethal cost of what happened to wives forced to contend with the whims of a king. At the age of eight or nine, she'd told Robert Dudley, who was to become the Earl of Leicester, that she would never marry.

It was Robert Dudley himself who came closest to bringing her to the altar. They'd been childhood friends when Robert was a playmate of her brother Edward's, and it had been Robert's father who had made a grab for power by marrying Lady Jane Grey to Edward and setting her up as queen of England. Robert himself had led troops in support of this coup, and for this reason he ended up locked in the Tower of London when Mary claimed the throne. His time there coincided with Elizabeth's own imprisonment in the Tower, and their friendship and romance blossomed. By most accounts, he was the one great love of Elizabeth's life. She appointed him to a high position in her court, and shortly after taking the throne, had his bedchamber moved next to hers. Rumors of their clandestine meetings soon put paid to her reputation as the "Virgin Queen."

Quite possibly though, Dudley or no Dudley, she might never have been that anyway. There is a very real possibility that she had been physically assaulted by her stepfather, Thomas Seymour, starting from when she was just thirteen. If that hadn't extended to physical assault, it was certainly a disturbing pattern of harassment. Thomas, who was then married to Elizabeth's stepmother, Jane Seymour (Edward's mother), made a habit of coming into Elizabeth's chamber first thing in the morning to try to catch her in bed or in her nightclothes. Elizabeth took to getting dressed earlier and earlier, but at one point, he actually tore her nightgown away in strips.

Whether there was abuse beyond that isn't clear. But it is known that, as queen, Elizabeth was adamant that she didn't want any man to take power from her.

"I will have but one mistress and no master," she famously said. I can't fault that logic.

Still, though, that meant that she had no heir of her flesh and blood. And meanwhile, Margaret Tudor, Henry VIII's sister, had a grandchild in Scotland.

Well, not *technically* in Scotland.

Let's back up and go north of the English border for a moment.

James V of Scotland, the nephew of Henry VIII, had been a vast disappointment to his uncle. When Henry had first decided to chuck all that Catholicism stuff and set himself up as the head of the Church of England, he had found it a wee little bit inconvenient to have a Catholic Scotland, whose Church was still headed by the pope (now no longer Henry's pal) directly on his border where just about anyone at all could mass an invasion against him. Catholic France would have been a good candidate, for example. They'd had a treaty with Scotland since 1295 and James' queen was French. Henry suggested to James that, really, Scotland should follow England's example and forget about being Catholic.

James didn't even want to discuss it.

War broke out.

Henry sent troops—and Bibles—into Scotland. A pissed-off James sent close to 18,000 Scottish troops to England, which started well but ended in squabbling about who was in charge and a disastrous defeat. Some 1,200 Scottish prisoners were taken by the English after the battle of Solway Moss, including many of James' chief commanders, advisors, and nobles.

James V died only six days after his daughter, Mary Stuart, was born. That made her the queen of Scots, but obviously she couldn't rule when she was barely old enough to drool. Immediately, she became the center of a tug-of-war for power that lasted most of her life.

First, there was the matter of who should be the regent until the young queen was able to govern for herself. Here, already, there were differences of allegiance between Scottish nationalists—those who wanted greater union with England—and those who looked to France. There was even a forged (probably) will, allegedly written by Mary's father James V, which Henry Beaton, the Archbishop of St.

Andrews and the last Scottish Cardinal before the Reformation, trotted out to support his claim to be Mary's regent. Which, in turn, got him thrown into prison. Which, in another turn, upset the pope.

In retaliation, the pope ordered that all churches in Scotland should be closed and no one could receive the sacraments.

Big mistake. Huge.

People needed their faith.

And remember those Bibles that Henry VIII had been giving out?

In a way, the pope played right into Henry's hands.

To further his consolidation of England and Scotland, Henry had decided that the new queen of Scots should marry his son Edward. Being magnanimous, he suggested, Mary could stay in Scotland until she reached the ripe old age of ten, if she absolutely had to, although to better prepare her for life as an English queen, she would need—obviously— *English* (and Protestant) people around her. Then from the age of ten, she would need to come and live in England until she was ready to get married.

Sounds like a great plan, doesn't it? From a Scottish perspective? Never mind Mary having no say in this at all.

As the Provost of Edinburgh, who was an advisor to Mary's regents, put it:

> "If your lad was a lass, and our lass were a lad, would you then be so earnest in this matter? ... And lykewise I assure you that our nation will never agree to have an Englishman king of Scotland. And though the whole nobility of the realm would consent, yet our common people, and the stones in the street would rise and rebel against it."

But there were split allegiances. The dangers of opposing Henry. Possible advantages.

Consequences.

And remember those Scottish prisoners? As the Scottish Parliament was contemplating Henry's proposal, Henry released many of them to go and help Parliament reach a smart decision on the subject of Mary's marriage. But he first required them to send "pledges"—usually family members—to take their places in England.

From Henry's perspective, at least, the Scottish

Parliament eventually came to the right conclusion.

But the Earl of Arran—Mary's regent, the Governor and Lord Protector of Scotland, and next in line to the throne if something happened to Mary—waffled on the implementation. Although he'd been a Protestant and part of the pro-English faction initially, he began to have his doubts. After meeting with the Archbishop of St. Andrews in secret, he converted to Catholicism and backed the pro-French "Auld Alliance" in favoring a marriage for Mary with the son of the king of France.

Henry now began a systematic proposal campaign that came to be called the "Rough Wooing." Don't let the name fool you.

It was war. Again. And again.

Civil war among the pro-English and pro-French factions in Scotland, between Protestants and Catholics.

War with Henry.

Then, too, there were all those Scottish prisoners and the "pledges" Henry had collected back in England. Pressure that Henry had no compunction in bringing to bear on the members of the Scottish Parliament.

No sooner did the Scottish Parliament renege on their approval of Henry's proposal when Henry called in the pledges, demanding the return to England of twenty of the highest-ranking prisoners, or they would face retribution against their family members. This bought him some support, or at least reluctance.

Next, he marched on Scotland outright. He burned and looted Edinburgh, sending the spoils away by ship while the army went south again, burning everything in its path.

The Scots rallied and won the Battle of Ancrum Moor, achieving a brief peace afterward, until some pro-English Scottish lords murdered the Archbishop of St. Andrews and set the whole thing off again. The French stepped in. Mary was whisked off to safety in France in 1547, newly engaged to the French Dauphin, the heir to the French throne, and French troops remained in France to help protect her throne.

Because don't think that the whole Mary-has-a-claim-to-the-English-throne things was lost on the king of France. Nope.

The moment Elizabeth I took the first steps to claiming the throne on her sister Mary's death, the king of France proclaimed Mary Queen of Scots to be the new queen of England—and oh, by the way, that made his son the king. He even ordered new silverware for the couple with the English coat of arms quartered alongside those of France and Scotland.

Elizabeth, obviously, liked this not so much. Shortly afterward, probably at least partially in an effort to underscore the futility of her being assassinated by English agents—Mary eventually signed a document leaving her claim to the thrones of both Scotland and England to France, which riled up the Scots to the point of an uprising. But first, Henry II of France died in a joust, and he was succeeded by Mary's husband, Francis.

Now Mary was queen of both Scotland and France, which added coupled to her claim to the English throne made her quite the threat. But she was still only sixteen, and, therefore, Scotland was still a regency overseen by Mary's French mother with support from French troops on the ground in Scotland.

Elizabeth, not loving the implications of any of this, and needing to block the French influence on her own border, quietly helped stoke unrest against Mary by supporting the rise of Protestant lords in Scotland and that of John Knox, a fiery Protestant preacher, who was both anti-Catholic and anti-French—which made him adamantly anti-Mary. Knox even (at least he's the most probable source) gave rise to a legend about her father, James V, prophesying on his deathbed that Mary would be the end of the Stewart/Stuart dynasty.

"It cam wi' a lass and it will gang wi' a lass!" he supposedly said, on learning that his wife Margaret had given birth to a daughter instead of a son.

Protestant influence in Scotland had continued to grow, and along with it, the power increasingly shifted away from Mary's mother as regent. The Protestants invited Elizabeth to send English troops to come and help them take control, and meanwhile an uprising of French Protestants made it impossible for France to send more troops to secure Mary's throne. This wasn't entirely successful, but by the time Mary finally arrived in Scotland the following year to take full control as queen, Scottish power sat in the hands of Protestant nobles backed by Queen Elizabeth, and the Scottish Parliament laid out a national Presbyterian church, the Church of Scotland or "Kirk."

Now with a Catholic queen and a Presbyterian church, Scotland was a nation divided by more than the usual issues that had plagued the interactions between the Highlands and the Lowlands.

Mary tried to regain control. She had a lot of personal charm and magnetism—not to mention that she was beautiful and nearly six feet tall—that she brought to bear in statecraft. Not for nothing was she known as "the fair devil of Scotland." But she didn't have the harsh lessons in politics that had characterized Elizabeth's childhood, and hers was an altogether more trusting and open nature. She had tremendous kindness and empathy, and though she was intelligent and educated in her own right, her education had not been as extensive or rigorous as Elizabeth's, either. Instead, she knew her own limitations and she made the mistake of thinking she could rely on the wisdom of advisors to make up any shortcomings in her own knowledge or experience. Coupled with her youth and tremendous power, this made her vulnerable to manipulation. And because she was reluctant, at first, to stamp down hard the way that Elizabeth and Mary had done, her sense of fair play was easily painted to the advantage of her foes.

But with a bit of help from interested parties, namely Elizabeth, John Knox, and Mary's own illegitimate—and Protestant—half-brother, Mary Stuart's efforts to elevate Catholics and secure her throne were viewed as the first steps in a new wave of anti-Protestantism. Fear spread that Mary would treat non-Catholics much the way that Bloody Mary had treated them. The fact that she confined her efforts to breakaway Protestant leaders didn't actually do that much to buy her any credit with her opponents, and instead, her failure to bring down those leaders actually harmed her cause with many Catholic lords.

Then, too, there were other reasons why not even all the Scots, much less all the English, supported Mary.

First, again egged on by Knox, many Scots, having become increasingly conservative, also objected to her flamboyant manner of dressing.

Second, with the death of her French husband a few months earlier, her French support had waned—France didn't have as much of a stake in the outcome anymore since they would no longer inherit her throne. Mary was, therefore, penalized by being seen as too French in the eyes of some, without a French army at her back.

Next, she made a disastrous second marriage. Lord Darnley was, like Mary herself, a grandchild of Margaret Tudor, the sister of Henry VIII. When they married, this effectively made them a double threat to Elizabeth, because both had a claim to the English throne. He was also Catholic. And, as an English subject, Elizabeth felt he should have asked her for permission before marrying, so it further alienated Elizabeth. Mary's Protestant half-brother, Moray, perceiving the union of two Catholics on the throne of Scotland, now also took up arms. That didn't come to much, but ultimately, Darnley proved more malleable than Mary, and he was encouraged to make a grab for the throne himself, allying with the Protestant lords against her. Once more, that came to nothing, but it didn't exactly do wonders for their marriage. Eventually, Darnley was murdered, though, and a whisper campaign against Mary began, accusing her and her alleged lover for being behind it.

Whether the Earl of Bothwell ever was Mary's lover before the murder is a question, and whether he actually murdered Darnley is also unclear. But he did kidnap her after the fact, and quite possibly by force, married her in a Protestant ceremony days after divorcing his former wife. In the eyes of Catholics, this made the marriage doubly unpopular. And Mary already had many enemies among both Protestants and the pro-England factions. The marriage, coming on top of the murder, gave them ammunition. In addition, the marriage was unhappy, and Mary suffered deep depression.

Soon, her enemies raised an army against her and Bothwell. She marshaled forces of her own, but many in her army deserted during the long negotiations with the opposing side, leaving her without sufficient strength to fight. Bothwell was allowed to slink away by the victorious Protestant lords, but they took Mary prisoner on charges of adultery and murder and marched her to Edinburgh beneath a banner sewn with a scene of the murdered Darnley dead beneath a tree while crowds jeered her en route. Eventually, she was forced to abdicate in favor of her son, and the Earl of Moray, her Protestant half-brother, was named as regent. Bothwell, meanwhile, went blithely into exile.

All of this ultimately had disastrous consequences—at least if you happened to believe that Scotland and England shouldn't be governed by one monarch, and a single set of laws, from London.

Mary managed to escape Scottish custody and fled south to England. This both put her into the power of Elizabeth and made her a rallying point for dissident Scots and Irish, which in turn spurred various plots against Elizabeth, some backed also by the king of Spain, who had made it his mission to become the defender of the Catholic faith. The Scots continued fighting on Mary's behalf. And Elizabeth and others eventually seized on this as a way to eliminate a rival with plausible deniability.

After a trial riddled with dubious evidence, Mary was executed for treason, and displayed such courage, dignity, and kindness at her execution that history has since treated her with a bit less bias. Even by her enemies, her kindness and beauty were famous. Adding to her tragic legend, her dog, a small Skye terrier, was hiding among her skirts at her execution. He was so devoted to her that he refused to be separated from her body until he was forcibly removed to have Mary's blood washed away.

(Mary's fondness for Scottish shortbread, which is attributed to her, features in *Magic of Winter*, so there's a recipe for that included in the recipe section of this book.)

With a single stroke—or rather three, because they didn't even manage to cut off Mary's head cleanly on the first try—Elizabeth consolidated the influence of the English crown over Scotland as well as England, Wales, and Ireland. Mary's son James took his mother's death without protest and became Elizabeth's heir, which eventually paved the way for the Acts of Union that created a single monarchy in Great Britain. James was, needless to say, raised a Protestant.

So much for Scotland. Armies had been unleashed against each other. Protestants against Catholics. Highlands against the Lowlands. New resentments began a slow bubble.

But Ireland's troubles were about to boil over.

The Determined Queen

"Men fight wars,
Women win them."

QUEEN ELIZABETH I

OUTSIDE THE PALE OF IRELAND, the Irish chieftains remained discontented and rebellious. Elizabeth's Protestant advisors urged her to be firmer in dealing with Catholics and the Irish in general, but she was—at first—reluctant to stir up what could become a full-scale revolt that would push even more Irish Catholics to conspire, like Shane O'Neill, with Scotland and France, or into open rebellion like Grace O'Malley, the O'Malley chief and "pirate queen" who became a lifelong thorn in Elizabeth's (and England's) side.

Elizabeth did impose some tighter measures on the Irish from the first, and she sent more troops to win the peace.

This only backfired.

Seeing opportunities under the anti-Irish laws of the Parliament of Ireland, these army captains and officials made things worse by stirring up the chieftains to revolt and then seizing their lands for themselves. (Sound familiar? It's the same technique allegedly used by the Earl of Argyll against the MacGregors.)

As the English troops increasingly cracked down—in many cases without Elizabeth's knowledge or consent for their policies—strange bedfellows began to come together. Irish chiefs allied themselves with different factions of "Old English" lords from within the Pale, most of whom were Catholic. Spanish and even Italian troops began to be put in play.

Elizabeth couldn't have that. Following the Desmond Rebellion, she sent a massive troop presence—the equivalent of shock and awe—into Ireland and laid waste to Munster in the North.

Enter the Ulster confederacy, which ushered in the Nine Years' War, also known as Tyrone's Rebellion. Hugh O'Neill, Earl of Tyrone, preached a religious and nationalist message that drew the attention of Irish chiefs and a bit of Old English support. They then paid to raise a sizable army of mercenaries and volunteers strong enough to counter

Elizabeth's own formidable forces, forcing her to spend more and more money, nearly bankrupting the English treasury and amounting to 19 percent of English overall manpower—more than 30,000 men.

As the war dragged on, Elizabeth became more determined to win, and increasingly brutal—some would argue genocidal—in policies that amounted to ethnic cleansing. The archaeology and history in my *Echo of Glory* (March, 2018) centers on the tail end of Tyrone's Rebellion, featuring an excavation on modern-day Dursey Island off the coast of the Beara Peninsula. It was on Dursey where the O'Sullivan massacre took place in 1602 that resulted in the deaths of 400 elderly, women, and children, who were butchered on orders from Elizabeth's commander. An additional 1,000 men, women, and children were driven north later that year on a long winter death march from Beara to Leitrim, where Donal Cam O'Sullivan Beare continued to wage a guerrilla war until just weeks before Elizabeth's death. (More about that later, too.)

Foreigners and Thieves

"May it please the king of Miracles
that we might see
if we only live a week therafter
Gráinne Mhaol and a thousand warriors
routing all the foreigners!"

PÁDRAIG PEARSE
"ÓRÓ SÉ DO BHEATHA 'BHAILE"

B ACK TO THE REIGN of James I of England and Ireland
(James V of Scotland), Mary Stuart's son.

With Elizabeth having succeeded in forcing the
surrender of Hugh O'Neill and the Flight of the Earls from
Ireland to seek new help from Spain for a further rebellion,
James was able to withdraw most of the troops. But with less
support from the old English-Irish aristocracy, he needed
fresh blood and tougher laws to keep control and keep the
peace. He proceeded to give away more Irish land, Irish
titles, and Irish wealth to English and Scottish Protestants,

escalating the prior practice known as "plantation," and increasing the Penal Laws.

In the northern counties of Ireland, which were almost entirely Catholic and Irish-speaking—and had been among the most rebellious, with additional worrisome ties to the insurgent Scottish Highlands—the Ulster Plantation saw wholesale colonization. The entire Irish population was supposed to be moved out, replaced by Presbyterian Scots and English Protestants who were specifically not allowed to take on Irish tenants or hire Irish workers. Instead, they had to import a minimum of forty-eight English speaking, Protestant men, at least twenty families, from England and Scotland, and they had to build defenses against the native Gaelic Irish. English soldiers and captains who had fought in the Nine Years' War were also given land.

The Ulster Plantation cast a long shadow. It's why Northern Ireland is still British. But plantation occurred in many stages, many areas, and many degrees.

Songs like *"Óró Sé Do Bheatha 'Bhaile"* ("Oh, Welcome Home"), originally a Jacobite song, was rewritten by the nationalist poet Pádraig Pearse before the Easter Rising of 1916, referring to thieves and foreigners taking Irish land and the Irish rising to take it back. It was sung by the Irish

Volunteers during the Irish War of Independence (1919 to 1921) and is still recorded and sung, with fantastic versions available by Sinead O'Connor and Seo Lin, among others.)

Plantation encompassed more than private land. Virtually all the lands and churches that had previously belonged to the Catholic Church were granted to the Protestant Church of Ireland, the Irish version of the Church of England, so that English clerics could begin converting the Irish Catholics.

This was all designed to ensure that English law, English citizens, and the English view of the church would be undisputed—oh, and not incidentally, and so that Catholic monarchs in Europe would find it harder to get a toehold within striking distance of English interests. On the ground, though, the practice of Reformation wasn't quite as complete as it had been envisioned.

Loyalty, family, determination, ingenuity, hard work, and simple humanity can't be ordered away so easily. By the English design, the native Irish were meant to move into specific areas, where they could be contained and guarded, but in practice, some were able to find less fertile land where they could eke out an existence. Friendships and enmities rose and fell, people were helped or betrayed. Human nature didn't change. The newcomers were merely different people, and—in the Irish view—they didn't belong. From the perspective of the incomers, they were doing what they had legally been asked by their King—they were "colonists" in Ireland, no different from their countrymen who were colonizing America at Jamestown (named after this King James) and seeking a better life among the "savages."

So, in Ireland—much like America—there was a fundamental difference of opinion about who had a right to be there. And though the people of Scotland had once been Gaels, many of those who now moved to Ireland were lowland Scots who'd already been incomers to Scotland. More importantly, many were Presbyterian or Puritan—not just Protestant—and some were quite hardline. Their religious outlooks had been hard-won, with years of secular and religious leaders killing each other on all sides, burning each other at the stake or killing each other in various new and fabulous ways, whipping up public sentiment against the other side in an endless loop. Their views were often aggressively black and white and fundamentally different than those of Irish Catholics.

Still, in many cases, people managed to find common ground in defiance of the English plan. Many of the Irish managed to not only survive, but to trade, fish, and farm—though the land they scraped together for themselves wasn't as fertile as the land they'd had before.

Rather than eradicating Catholicism entirely, the English plan drove the religion largely underground. Private Catholic services were overlooked. And trouble quietly continued brewing.

At home in England, meanwhile, James—known as the "Wisest Fool in Christendom"—took steps to reconcile the more Calvinist Scottish "Kirk" with the Anglican Church of England. Leaving in place a Calvinist theology that let the Scots worship as before, he put a more Anglican Church government in place. He was also, however, responsible for what's known today as the king James Bible, the version of the Christian Bible "authorized" for the Church of England.

Simultaneously, James sparked the "witch-hunts" and personally supervised the torture of women accused of witchcraft. (Note, if you watch your mother's execution without reacting, what does that say about you? What does it *do* to you?)

Next came Charles I. Like his father, Charles was a strong believer in the "divine right of kings," which he took as license to do whatever the heck he wanted, including raising taxes without approval or consent from Parliament. He restored power to many Catholics and further reformed church practices, but in a way that many people, especially in Calvinist-leaning Scotland, thought was coming too close to Catholicism. This, along with his reckless spending, made him wildly unpopular.

Things didn't often fare well for unpopular kings.

War of Three Kingdoms

"There isn't a tree to hang a man,
water to drown a man,
nor soil to bury a man."

ANON. ENGLISH OFFICER IN IRELAND

R EBELLION ERUPTED AGAIN IN Ireland in 1640, and from
1639 to 1649, Charles I fought Scottish and English
armies in the first English Civil War, the beginning of what
was known as the Wars of the Three Kingdoms.

The problem was, once again, how far Reformation
should go.

By now, there were many different flavors of
Protestantism. The most similar to Catholicism was still the
Church of England, and this was favored by Charles as a
more uniform, ordered, and traditional style. By more
Calvinist and Lutheran Protestants, Presbyterians, and

Puritans, these same elements were arguably "papish" and corrupt.

Also, reforms proposed by Charles in an attempt to impose a structure and hierarchy on the Presbyterian churches and make them more ecclesiastical and "English" in the way they were governed was seen by protestors as taking power from the people. Many opposed any effort to revert back from the populist reforms that had made religion, finally, accessible to the common people. Over the years, the Presbyterian sects had removed the traditional church structures that kept power in the hands of a select few, and they'd advocated for education so that people could read the Bible for themselves.

This sounds great in principle, but in many cases, it led to a harsh interpretation and an environment in which people felt emboldened to take it upon themselves to police the behavior and faith of their neighbors. Public shaming and harsh punishments, including whipping and cropping of the ears, were commonplace for blasphemy, laziness, vanity, drunkenness, smoking, and fornication. People grew more outspoken, and they were passionate about their religion and their right to practice it as they saw fit. This suppressed personal choice and freedoms, and it also led to women being viewed as more subservient and inferior to men, doomed to carry the stain of Eve's original sin.

This was the atmosphere that had led to the start of the witch trials. Something not going well? Blame a woman. Seek a common enemy. Be united in your anger against someone else.

And Charles I, having once again moved to reconcile the religious practices in the Scotland Kirk with those of Church of England, ran afoul of this. After he introduced new bishops and a new style of prayer book, riots erupted in the streets of Edinburgh.

Resistance continued with the Covenanters.

Remember John Knox, the fiery preacher who contributed to the downfall of Mary Queen of Scots?

The Covenanters were devoted followers of his teachings and those of John Calvin. They organized fresh opposition and took an oath of resistance—the National Covenant of 1638—swearing to "Defend the true religion and recover the purity and liberty of the Gospel." A few months later, these "Covenanters" deposed the bishops and did away with the government of Charles' more "papish" church.

Again, take all this with a grain of salt. Emotions tended to run high, and each side vilified the other.

Anyway, much back and forth ensued. There was killing all around.

In Scotland, the centuries-old rivalry between the Campbells and the Grahams pitted the eighth Earl of Argyll, a Campbell, and the Marquess of Montrose, a Graham, against each other. The Grahams had always been Royalists, and once again, they backed Charles I. The Campbells had done a pretty fair job—on many— occasions of backing *themselves*, which was not unusual among the high-placed families. And this time was no different. The Earl of Argyll managed to get himself elevated to Marquess, and arguably came close to being dictator of Scotland. In the process, his old enemy, the Marquess of Montrose, was hanged and dismembered, and his head was impaled on a spike, where it remained, slowly rotting away, for the next eleven years.

Next, leading the Covenanters, Argyll sent an army of experienced men into England and to Ireland. Charles tried to raise an army on his own without support from Parliament, which he was having trouble getting. Eventually, the Covenanters captured Charles and handed him over to the English Parliament, which by now had a significant Puritan faction.

A believer in the divine right of kings to the end, Charles refused, even after his ultimate surrender and captivity, to agree to the demands of the Parliament to form a constitutional monarchy and curb his religious meddling. He managed to escape briefly, and made peace with Argyll and the Scots, but in the meantime along came Oliver Cromwell.

With a borrowed name and one distant and very wealthy relative, Oliver Cromwell developed ambition early in his life. And that led him, in a series of increasingly brutal steps, to amass more power than any king in England had yet wielded.

In a way, perhaps, it goes back to Henry VIII again. Among the not insignificant number of people that Henry VIII had beheaded was one Thomas Cromwell, who had risen to become his chief minister before falling out of favor. Thomas' sister, trying to elevate her family, chose to use the Cromwell name and to give it to her own children instead of using her married name of Williams. And maybe not insignificantly, given Oliver's later actions, Thomas Cromwell managed to take for himself and his family a property that had once belonged to the Catholic Church as a monastery. This became the family seat, and Oliver's grandfather, Sir Henry Cromwell, was one of the richest men in the district.

But Oliver's branch of the family were poor relations. His own father, though he used the name Cromwell, was a second son, and Oliver grew up in a modest townhome until his father moved them to the country and took up farming on a small bit of land.

From an early age, Cromwell developed a strange relationship with the church, both a fascination with and a hatred of wealth and power, a deep sense of inequality, and a hatred for bishops and "papishness." He was educated locally and his extremist views continued to grow. On his father's death, with seven unmarried sisters and his mother to support, he left college and returned home to take up the family farm.

It was there that he first began to suffer periods of deep depression. But he continued his own education in between work, and he even briefly studied law in London, where he met his wife whose wealthy family had some ties to Puritanism. By the 1630s, Oliver had not only become a Puritan himself, he had become convinced that he was chosen to be an instrument of God in setting the world's wrongs to right.

This he set out to do with single-minded determination and the belief that nothing was off limits in his quest. With Machiavellian resolve, he cut down anyone who stood in his way and destroyed anyone close to them as well. And despite often being portrayed as a man of humble means who clawed his way to the top, Cromwell's rise only began when he inherited wealth from his maternal uncle, and along with it a constituency in Cambridge.

His rise in Parliament didn't occur until his second session, by which time the country was in turmoil and ears were willing to hear the particular brand of extremism that Cromwell had come to believe. In Parliament, he spoke out against King Charles, the Church of England, and—most especially—against Charles' policies in Scotland that had resulted in a humiliating English defeat. The more Charles butted heads with Parliament, the more popular views of men like Cromwell became.

Two years later, when war broke out between Charles and the Parliament, Cromwell took hold of the opportunity with both hands. In command of a small, untrained armed force, he distinguished himself on the battlefield with a combination of luck, strategic talent, and an ability to bully and cajole his "Ironsides" into fighting for him with lethal effectiveness inspired by the belief that they were battling in the name of God. In 1644, the troops under his command were instrumental in annihilating a royalist force and earned Cromwell a nearly fervent following after the Battle of Marston Moor.

In 1649, his personal power had grown to the point where he was one of the men who signed the death warrant that authorized King Charles' execution.

For most men, that would have been a deeply solemn thing. Certainly not one to be taken lightly. Most of the men lived with that decision with difficulty.

Indecision was never one of Cromwell's problems. Including and beyond regicide, he was quick to capitalize on every opportunity.

With Charles dead, he amassed ever-increasing power for himself. He continued destroying abbeys, convents, monasteries, and churches. He warred with anyone who'd tried to defend the monarchy or the earlier Church of England or Catholic establishment. Priests were hunted down or hid in priest holes that were specifically built in the great houses to shelter them. While he's sometimes been portrayed as a liberator or a populist, he didn't believe in rights for people in general—only for the "godly."

The beheading of Charles I led to even more power. Royalists recognized Charles' eldest son, Charles II, as king of England, Ireland, and Scotland, and Charles was crowned King of Scotland in 1641, but he was never able to retake England, and Cromwell soon routed him and sent him fleeing to exile in France. (Cromwell and the escape of Charles II, along with the general history of St. Michael's Mount in Cornwall, is the subject of *Bell of Eternity*, since that resulted in the loss of the legendary abbey bell in the story.)

Cromwell, meanwhile, became Lord Protector of the Commonwealth in 1653, wielding as much if not more power than any king in English history. He didn't wield it kindly.

In the most brutal military campaigns ever conducted against Scotland and Ireland, he swept away centuries of tribal power and custom. Ireland was a particular target. Many there, despite years of efforts to the contrary, had remained stubbornly Catholic, and Cromwell not only hated that, but he saw the possibility of Ireland being used as a point of invasion from Catholic France or Spain in support of Royalist forces. He personally commanded the Confederate Wars there in 1649 and 1650, and finally defeated the Confederate and Royalist coalition. His policies and actions against Irish Catholics were blatantly genocidal—up to one-fifth of the country's total population was killed on his command. And the final defeat of the Royalist coalition there resulted in still more penalties against the Irish and years of suffering.

But Cromwell didn't ignore Scotland entirely. Between 1650 and 1651, he fought there as well, happily butchering Catholics, and he was at times punitive in England and Wales (which was part of England then) as well.

In 1653, he forcibly set aside the Rump Parliament of which he was a member, and set up the Barebone's Parliament, which he later disbanded completely. Having gotten rid of the monarchy and the Parliament, in effect, he then became Lord Protector of England, Scotland, and Ireland, and governed as brutally and effectively as a dictator. He died in 1658 and the Parliament invited Charles II, the eldest son of the executed Charles I, to come back from France and retake the throne.

Royalists swept back into power, whereupon they dug up and beheaded Oliver Cromwell's corpse. Presumably, they spat upon it, too. Or maybe not. I think cutting off its head probably conveyed their contempt pretty clearly.

His head was found by a soldier, who hid it away in his chimney for many years then willed it to his daughter. Years later, people marveled at it in a freak show with a sign that proclaimed it as "the Monster's head."

The Killing Time

WHILE FRANCE WAS STILL a Catholic country, Charles had managed to remain a Protestant. But this wasn't entirely enough. Many of his subjects still held Puritan or deeply independent and conservative views. And that embroiled him right back into fresh religious conflicts.

Now, we're back to the Covenanters again. Remember how the Scots had accepted Charles II as the rightful king of Scotland almost from the moment his father had been executed by the English?

Oh, wait. There'd been one small catch.

Before he'd been able to enter Scotland to be crowned, the Marquess of Argyll ("Argyll the Grim") and the Covenanters had first insisted that Charles II had to take oaths accepting Presbyterianism as the religion throughout Britain and Ireland.

Which Charles had done, because he needed the support of the Covenanters against the forces of the English Parliament. Only then he'd spent some time in Scotland having his youthful conduct and inclinations endlessly examined and held up to standards of conduct in which he had never been raised, and then being lectured by sober (and sometimes self-serving or even hypocritical) Presbyterians about his many failings.

Charles hadn't actually enjoyed any of that, and what with one thing or another—including the very real possibility of his head ending up on the end of Oliver Cromwell's pike—he'd taken himself off to exile in Catholic France, where he'd spent the intervening years quietly seething over the fact that his father's head had been cut off and that he himself had been deprived of his rightful throne.

Ten years later, on being restored to the Crown, having lived in the excitement of the Court of France and now facing the prospect of living once again with the restrictive

Presbyterian limitations on virtually everything that he considered fun, he wasn't finding the prospect of being king in a Covenanter format much fun.

Not only did he renege on his promise of making Presbyterianism universal, he also overthrew the Presbyterian church structure in Scotland and made anyone taking public office in Scotland reject the Covenants that had rolled back his father's efforts to reestablish an orderly hierarchical structure in the Church of Scotland. Furthermore, he made them swear not to take up arms against him.

And if anyone didn't like it? Tough. For example, ministers and clerics who didn't accept that situation lost their right to preach in church. Many didn't accept. Instead, a worrisome number chose to preach in open fields instead, and some attracted thousands of followers, many of them armed and dangerous to the Crown. Some of these meetings frankly became less about prayer and faith than they did about a fresh round of rebellion.

Afraid of losing control, the newly reestablished church government backed by the Crown fined anyone who didn't attend an officially-sanctioned church. Lowland militia and companies of armed Highlanders under men like the

Viscount Dundee—son of the executed Marquess of Montrose—were quartered in Covenanter territories in an effort to keep the peace. But as had so often happened in the past, an army let loose on a civilian population didn't actually help anything.

Over the next few years, this led to fresh armed rebellions. And a few more battles. And the assassination of the head of the Church of Scotland.

Oh, and the Marquess of Argyll? He was both the first Marquess and the last. This Grim Argyll's skill at protecting his family fortunes finally came to a gradual end with the ascendance of Oliver Cromwell. His power waned, and by the time Charles II was restored to the throne, Argyll was weak and heavily mired in debt.

Which, for the devilishly clever Campbells, was surprising.

Now, to be fair, the Campbells weren't the only clan who had learned to play to their own self-interests. Maintaining power and walking the bloody and brutal dagger's edge of the long struggles between Scotland and England, between warring religious factions, and between Crown and religion, was only really survivable if you hedged your bets. In many powerful families, in Scotland as well as elsewhere, the head of a family might fight on one side while his son fought on the opposite. This allowed the family to argue allegiance to the winner of a conflict no matter who actually won and, in this way, to manage to keep a grasp on the family wealth and land.

The Campbells had gotten very good at this through the years, so while the Marquess of Argyll had been leading Scotland on behalf of the Covenanters, his son had planted himself squarely on the Royalist side.

The higher one flies, though, the farther one has to crash.

With Charles II back on the throne, the younger Campbell had found himself in favor at Charles' court. Argyll the Grim? Not so much. Oh, he tried. He presented himself to Charles II intending to give him the whole remember-when-I-crowned-you-king speech, but he found himself summarily whisked back to Edinburgh instead with a charge of treason hung around his neck for his part in having Charles I beheaded.

Argyll seemed to have more political lives than a cat, though, and for a time, it appeared he might manage to talk himself out of a guilty verdict. Only he'd amassed a lot of enemies—a lot. A whole lot. In addition to Charles II himself, there were all the friends of the former Marquess of

Montrose and the Graham clan. Montrose, quite apart from having remained loyal to the Crown, had managed to make himself a genuine folk hero through his bravery and his dashing personal style. Even while being led to the gallows, he'd infuriated the Grim Argyll by commanding the respect and tears of the type of crowd who usually came out to cheer a good public execution. Then, too, there were a host of MacDonalds—former Lords of the Isles from whom the Campbells had seized land, wealth, and power. The Gordons, Ogilvies, MacLeans, MacDougalls, and of course, the MacGregors, all had hereditary grudges of their own. On top of that, there were the grudges that Grim Argyll had amassed himself in the way he treated those around him, those who owed him debts, and those to whom he owed debts in turn.

Just when Argyll was seeing hope for acquittal, one of those enemies produced letters Argyll had written—letters proving collusion between Argyll and Oliver Cromwell. Well, that was the end of Argyll. He was executed before Charles II even had time to sign his death warrant, and his head was impaled on the same spike on which, for the past eleven years, the Marquess of Montrose's skull had gruesomely overlooked the city.

None of which made the general situation in Scotland any calmer.

In 1680, the Covenanters issued a public declaration that the people of Scotland refused to accept the authority of a king who didn't keep his oaths and wouldn't recognize their religion.

They also opposed the succession of Charles II's brother James, who was the heir apparent to the throne. More importantly, having been raised in France, like Charles, James had been exposed to Catholicism. In fact, despite having been raised in and still professing loyalty to the Church of England, he had secretly converted.

With no legitimate children (the word "legitimate" is important here) of his own, Charles had always encouraged James to keep a low profile on any religious non-conformity, and to make certain he raised his daughters Mary and Anne as Protestants. Which James had.

On the restoration of the monarchy, Charles brought James back to England and continued grooming him to be his heir. He elevated him to the titles Duke of York, an English title, and Duke of Albany, a Scottish title. He was given governmental functions, in which he displayed greater work ethic, aptitude, and leadership abilities than Charles himself, having been an officer in both the French and Spanish militaries. Charles also granted him colonies in America, and James is the one after whom New York is named. (Maryland is named after his mother.)

Since James had kept his religious conversion private, few had initially known whether he was Catholic. Charles was known to lean too far in that direction—certainly, he was far too much of a libertine and engaged in too many vices to be a good Protestant, much less a Presbyterian. But James? Well, at least his behavior wasn't as bad as that of Charles. He was accepted fairly graciously at first, but they didn't much love his second wife, Mary of Modena, an Italian princess who many in Britain accused of being an actual agent of the pope.

Overall, with many people still dying because someone else considered them the wrong level or flavor of Protestant, the idea of a Catholic back on the throne—and of a long line of Catholic monarchs on the throne—was too horrific for many to bear. James was accused of various trumped-up things, including plotting to overthrow his brother, which all started to fuel anti-Catholic hysteria in England. In Scotland, it fired up many Presbyterians even more, and especially the Covenanters, whose quiet discussions about rebellion started to spill into action against Charles and James as his designated heir.

This had already been the case in England the previous year, when a movement to exclude James from the succession in favor of Charles' illegitimate son, the Duke of Monmouth, had been introduced in the English Parliament. The Exclusion Bill had nearly passed in the English Parliament in 1679, but Charles had stepped in and managed to avert the crisis. Afterward, he had instructed James to give up his administrative duties and go lie low somewhere.

Which James had done, or tried to do. But now the Covenanters had become so angry over the question of succession, and over Charles' religious policies, that they announced they would no longer accept—or consider—Charles II to be the rightful king of Scotland. Charles needed someone he could trust to step in, and he decided to make James High Commissioner of Scotland. He sent him off to suppress the uprising.

That could have ended really, really badly.

But James, while arrogant and impatient, was also generally effective, fair, and—being a bit more serious minded and willing to work than Charles—was more palatable to the Presbyterians. Surprisingly, he managed to make some allies, including the Viscount Dundee, a member of the powerful Graham family who had been staunchly Royalist supporters since the time of the first Scottish War of Independence.

On the other hand, he also made more enemies. Among these was the son of the Marquess of Argyll who—thanks to his loyalty to Charles II—had been restored to the land and titles of the former Earls of Argyll. The new earl had nevertheless found himself deeply in debt and had since set about trying to restore his fortunes—and renewing old feuds and hatching new ones.

The new earl's most powerful enemies soon included James and Charles himself. As hereditary Chief Justicular of the Highlands, Argyll returned to commanding a great deal of power—too much, in Charles' estimation, a fact that James conveyed to Argyll. To appease the royal brothers, Argyll signed an oath confirming his belief in the divine right of kings, but fell short of agreeing to convert to Catholicism at James' invitation in exchange for continued influence.

Meanwhile, back in England, while Charles was playing around and enjoying his own amusements, his advisors were quietly trying to pave the way for a smoother transition of leadership. A new Succession Act stipulated that the natural heir to the throne had rights thereto, regardless of religion, paving the way for a Catholic king once again. At the same time, though, the Scottish Test Act required that all public officials had to swear to the king but promise to uphold the Protestant religion. That meant that James *could* be king after Charles, but he couldn't, at least theoretically, mess with the balance of faith or power.

So far, so good.

Except that, in the meantime, the Duke of Monmouth, having gotten a tantalizing taste for power, didn't turn down the chance to participate in a fresh plot to overthrow the monarchy—again—and reinstitute a new Cromwellian-style government. This didn't turn out well for him, and the plotters were caught. Monmouth initially confessed, then took it back and proclaimed his innocence, and off he went into exile. James, and Charles, got the benefit of a bit of sympathy over it all, and Charles took advantage of this to bring James back from Scotland to serve on the Privy Council.

But all was not yet rosy for the royals. James' Protestant daughter, Mary, was quietly sent off to marry the Dutch (Protestant) prince, William of Orange, and she went to live in Holland. Remember this, because it's about to become important.

Charles II died in 1685 (and converted to Catholicism on his deathbed, fueling even more speculation and animosity in some quarters), and James was crowned. Few people knew for certain, yet, whether he was definitely Catholic, but—theoretically at least—the Succession Act made that okay anyway, so no one objected *terribly* much. Most people were more or less relieved to get a new king, especially one who seemed more capable of actually attending to the business of governing than Charles had been, without having to go around killing each other all over again to figure out who that king would be.

Being of a pragmatic nature, James even managed to pardon the people who had wanted to refuse him his rightful throne. Overcoming his pride, he was ready to get on with the business of governing.

But then . . .

Feeling entirely justified, James decided that Catholics—and Protestant nonconformists—might also deserve some forgiveness and religious freedom. Oh, and they should get to hold offices. High offices.

Scotland, especially, didn't like any of this. Their tolerance for James' own Catholicism didn't extend to a tolerance for Catholicism in general, and they were outraged. To quell the outcry, the Scottish Privy Council, acting on James behalf, authorized the killing—without trial—of anyone who refused to take an Oath of Abjuration, renouncing the Scottish National Covenant and swearing loyalty to the new Catholic king. This resulted in more than 100 executions within the first months after James took office.

Back in England as well, people—including Parliament and James' own daughters Anne and Mary—started muttering darkly about his Catholic leanings. Many considered his religious tolerance a violation of the Test Act that he had signed and of his coronation oath. The Privy Council and his advisors counseled him to stop pushing what could appear to be a pro-Catholic agenda, but the idea of anyone trying to limit his authority didn't sit well with James—any more than it had with his father and brother.

Charles II hadn't spent enough time in sober reflection to have much of an opinion about divine right, but like his grandfather, James believed implicitly that his authority derived directly from God. When he went ahead and tried to impose his new measures toward religious freedom, Parliament refused to approve them. James' response? Dissolve Parliament and go on without them.

This was *so* not a good plan. It led to many problematic things.

Whispers.

Plots.

Rebellions.

An eventual *coup d'etat* on the part of Parliament and the Prince of Orange.

The Duke of Monmouth, having spent time visiting Mary and William of Orange in Holland, returned to southern England and declared himself king. He tried to muster support, but people were ambivalent, and James defeated the small force he raised relatively easily. James executed him at the Tower of London.

Simultaneously, Archibald Campbell, the ninth Earl of Argyll, whose father's head had only recently replaced the Marquess of Montrose's head on a spike in Edinburgh, sailed back to Scotland and tried to raise a force to oppose James there. This seems to have been prompted by genuine concern for the welfare of Scotland and England, but it didn't go very well, either, and mostly it was only Archibald's own Campbell clansmen who fought beside him against Royalist forces. He was quickly defeated, tried, and executed.

(The Earl of Argyll here was the predecessor of the first Duke of Argyll, who would eventually shelter Rob Roy MacGregor and provide him with a shield against the next and newly more powerful Marquess of Montrose. The later Argylls were deeply esteemed, and though they continued to support the government side, even Bonnie Prince Charlie wrote in a letter to his father that he wished he could have Argyll's support.)

But that came later. First, let's go back to the ignominious downfall of James.

The Glorious Revolution

T HE ENGLISH PARLIAMENT HAD been aghast when King James II had proposed religious freedom. He next began filling high-level posts with Catholics. The way Parliament saw this, or at least claimed they saw it, the whole idea of religious freedom had been only a ruse James was using, the first step in reestablishing Catholicism as the primary religion.

By now in England and Scotland almost everyone had been taught that anything "papish" was tantamount to evil. They still feared a return to the policies of Bloody Mary (Mary Tudor), although what those policies might have been, as well as the number of deaths that could be laid at Mary's door, had become greatly exaggerated. Now to compound the hysteria, James had sent the members of Parliament home to their constituencies and, almost simultaneously, his young wife had finally given him a bouncing (Catholic) baby boy. Panic ensued. A rumor spread that the baby wasn't even royal—that a changeling had been smuggled into the birthing chamber in a warming pan when the real baby had been stillborn. James own daughter Anne fed into this fear by being absent from the birth. She wrote to her sister that she would never be satisfied whether the baby was "true or false."

Armed with the fear that a new Catholic line of monarchs was set to stake out the English throne and the slander about the substitute child, on top of their own loss of their own power, the members of Parliament ex-officially decided something had to be done. But what?

James wasn't entirely unaware of how the boat was leaning. The last king who had defied Parliament outright had quite literally lost his head, but, on the other hand, the way James saw it, he was king. *He*. Was. King. Divine right and all that. Why should he back down in doing something he was convinced was right just because Parliament had a difference of opinion?

The atmosphere around the palace became a little scary. Seeing the writing on the wall, James' wife disguised herself as a washerwoman and snuck the baby Charles away to France, where the bonnie young prince would—it turned out later—be raised in exile.

Meanwhile, the members of Parliament had decided they weren't taking all this lying down. So they fired off a polite invitation for James' daughter Mary and her safely Protestant husband to bring an invasion force to England.

Which they promptly did.

By now, James had lost nearly all of the support he'd had on ascending the throne, so this time when he tried to raise an army to fight for him, not only did he not get many takers, most of his regular army deserted.

The invasion by William and Mary is called the "Glorious Revolution" of 1688. In truth, it was neither very "Glorious" nor much of a "Revolution." Nor was it really about religion. The English Parliament saw an opportunity to keep their own power, Princess Anne contributed by being neither overly bright nor politically savvy, and William of Orange seized an opportunity to become King of England. In truth, William maintained a friendly(ish) relationship with the pope, and he had placed Catholics high within his own administration.

James fled to France for safety, and almost the moment he was out of the country, Parliament declared that he had abdicated. They gave the throne to Mary and William as co-monarchs of England and Ireland.

The question of Scotland wasn't as easily settled, though.

Only about two percent of Scots were Catholic at this point. There were a fair few who believed in the divine right of kings, though, and even more who didn't see why they should be ruled by a king from Holland. The king of England was only their king because he'd been King of Scotland first. And James was and—whatever his faults—remained, a Stuart. The Stuarts (previously Stewarts) had ruled in Scotland very nearly from the beginning of Scottish Independence after all—given Robert the Bruce's daughter's marriage. Between all that and the personal support he'd won earlier from people like Viscount Dundee, James had a small following who supported him over Mary and William. These supporters were hoping that the Scottish Parliament would choose to support him over the foreign king and queen.

Then he made a *big* mistake.

He sailed to Ireland, where he had built-in support. Despite all English efforts to the contrary, there were still a lot of Catholics left in Ireland. And the Irish had little reason to be loyal to Mary, much less to William.

En route to Ireland, he wrote a letter to the Scottish National Convention, whose support he needed. The letter was intended to convince them that, regardless of what England had done, they—the Scottish people—really wanted and needed him as king more than they wanted to settle for monarchs who were entirely foreign.

But James was prideful, hurt, angry, and afraid. As a result, in its uncanny ability to sound simultaneously demanding, self-aggrandizing, sniveling, and offensive, the letter is reminiscent of the Mr. Collins character in Jane Austen's *Pride and Prejudice*. And it didn't go over well.

The National Convention duly voted to accept William and Mary as their sovereigns.

Viscount Dundee and James supporters couldn't accept that. They called for loyal and Catholic clans to rally to the Stuart cause.

Some of them answered the call. At least in part. Sometimes.

But most in Scotland chose to see how things fell before wading into war on James' behalf. Even within families, they split into factions, some on religious grounds, some on what they stood to gain.

Memories are long in the Highlands, and that's where most—though not all—of the Jacobite support was found. Presbyterian clans like the MacLeans had old scores to settle with other clans. But keeping Highland forces together was hard at the best of times, and any sort of delay would cost support among those who answered the call. Bonnie Dundee and the scant forces he'd assembled pushed forward.

Devilish Bonnie Dundee

"To the Lords of Convention 'twas Clavers who spoke.
'Ere the king's crown shall fall there are crowns to be broke;
So let each Cavalier who loves honour and me,
Come follow the bonnet of Bonny Dundee."

SIR WALTER SCOTT
"BONNIE DUNDEE"

"BONNIE" DUNDEE, AS JOHN Graham, Laird of Claverhouse and first Viscount Dundee was also known, was a Protestant, though not a Presbyterian. His reputation in combat had also earned him the nickname "Bloody Clavers" among his enemies, although by most accounts he was actually a fair and very honorable man.

His military career began in the Scots Brigade, serving in the command of the Duke of Monmouth while fighting in Europe on behalf of the king of France. Alliances at that time were complicated, and during the short reign of James II and the longer period under his brother, King Charles II, Europe had been in turmoil. Outright war had broken out in 1688 between King Louis XIV of France and an uneasy coalition of the Holy Roman Empire, Spain, Austria, the Dutch Republic, Savoy, and England. Fought not only on the Continent, it spread to Ireland, India, and North America—and to the seas in between. In truth, it was the first "world war," and it provided opportunities for soldiers to earn money and advancement fighting in regiments like the Scots or Irish Brigades.

Ironically, the Duke of Monmouth whom Dundee served in that war was the same man—Charles II's illegitimate Protestant son—who later twice tried to overthrow Charles and James to set himself up as king in their place. In addition, while in the same Scots Regiment, Bonnie Dundee had saved the life of William of Orange, the Dutch prince, who the English Parliament later placed on James' throne. Dundee's wife was also the daughter of a Covenanter, so his determined allegiance to the Jacobite cause was all the more remarkable.

By all accounts, Dundee *was* handsome and dashing, but the name "Bonnie Dundee" that came to be attributed to him had already been applied to the city of "Dundee," so when he was made Constable of Dundee—and later Viscount Dundee—the nickname transferred to him quite easily. On returning to Scotland after his military service in Europe, he was tasked to help suppress the illegal outdoor churches that were being established by ministers who refused to submit to King Charles' attempts to establish a hierarchy in the church—meetings that were often used as cover by well-armed Covenanters to organize opposition to the king and his policies, and when Scotland rebelled against Charles and Charles sent James to Scotland to quash the uprising, Dundee and James briefly worked together. James later made him commander of all Scottish forces and called him to England when the forces of William of Orange were invading.

After losing in England, Bonnie Dundee carried the fight back to Scotland. This was, at first, a rhetorical fight. When a Convention of the Estates was held, the overwhelming control by Covenanters and pro-William supporters spurred Dundee and other Jacobite loyalists to mount a counter-convention in Stirling. This was foiled by a plot to murder Dundee, and he retired to his own estate at Dudhope, paving the way for the Edinburgh convention to give the Scottish crown to William and Mary in place of James.

But as far as Dundee—and other Jacobite loyalists—knew, James was still planning to come to Scotland. Believing that the tide would turn when James—who was also an experienced soldier and commander—left Ireland and came in person to rally supporters and lead the fight to restore his crown, Dundee traveled the length and breadth of the country, passionately persuading clans and soldiers, anyone who would listen, to take up arms beside them. In this, he was joined by men like Ewen Cameron of Lochiel, who with his "Cameronians" had also been trying to rally troops to support the beleaguered king despite most of the country being unwilling to really get behind either side in the conflict.

Waging a hard and often lonely battle both of words and arms, Dundee spent months trying to raise money, arms, and men through the Gordon and Atholl territories and elsewhere in the Highlands, while dodging, outwitting, and often downright fighting against the forces of General Mackey, who was in command of a mixed "government" army comprised of the Scottish Brigade from William of Orange's native Holland, English dragoons, and conscript—generally reluctant—Scots raised by levy.

Pursued as a traitor and hounded on every side, Dundee was run off his own properties. Opposing forces garrisoned in his own town of Dundee even shut the gates against him after he'd raised the king's standard outside the city to rally fighters to James' cause. Loyal cavalry and troops inside kept him from being arrested, but he had to retreat north to safety.

But ultimately, all Jacobite hopes of James coming to Scotland proved to be in vain. James never arrived. Mackay's army captured a main port, making it hard for even supplies to make it through from Ireland.

Still, Dundee and the Cameronians found some Jacobite support in Scotland. The Duke of Gordon held Edinburgh castle for James, and fighting men came from the Gordons, the MacNabs, the Cowals, the Gibbonses, and the MacGregors. In other instances, help came in the lack of active opposition, or divided family loyalties. The Marquess of Atholl—a Murray, by this time, and not a Campbell—laid siege to his own Blair Castle, a key strategic point controlling access to the Lowlands, which had been taken by his steward and handed to the Jacobite forces. (The Murray family was to be divided between government and Jacobite allegiances for many years to come.)

Then the tide turned again. The Duke of Gordon gave up Edinburgh. Mackay's sizable force pressed on.

Dundee, having finally received a few hundred reinforcements from Ireland as well as reinforcement at Blair Castle, saw an opportunity to catch Mackay, and he made yet another call for the clans to join him. Joined by the Lochiels and the Camerons, along with the Irish fighters, he took up a strategic position above the pass of Killicrankie, a narrow two-mile-long road with a steep slope on one side and the River Garry on the other. Through this pass, Mackay marched his 2,400 government troops.

The Jacobite rebels, less than half of the government numbers, were waiting.

Though Mackay's first volley of muskets against the Jacobite charge dropped 600 clansmen, the troops could not reload quickly enough. The Jacobites fired their own muskets, then charged with a furious onslaught of swords and axes that tore through the heart of the government formation. In less than thirty minutes, the battle was over and more than 2,000 of Mackay's government troops were dead. He himself escaped and watched the remaining action from the ridge, then proceeded on to Stirling.

But the battle had an enormous cost for the Jacobites as well, and for the Jacobite cause overall.

Disappointed at James' continued failure to leave Ireland and the recent loss of Edinburgh castle, Bonnie Dundee believed the Battle of Kincross was the last Jacobite hope— requiring nothing short of victory. He himself led the Highlanders in the first gallant, desperate charge against Mackay's muskets, and he died of his wounds.

With his death, the driving force of the Jacobite rebellion was broken, and while the Jacobites continued fighting briefly under Alexander Cannon, the first of the main pushes to restore the Stuart monarchy came to end. In August of 1691, James gave permission for his supporters to surrender and negotiate for whatever personal pardons they could get from England.

Such was the hysteria and propaganda of the time that it was widely reported that, having made a pact with the devil, Bonnie Dundee could not be killed by lead and had been struck down on the battlefield only because a silver button from his coat had been driven into his chest by the bullet's impact.

Treachery at Glencoe

"We gave him our food with a brother's own feeling;
for then we believed there was truth in Argyll."

MARY MAXWELL CAMPBELL
"LAMENT FOR GLENCOE"

EMORIES AND RIVALRIES RUN long, deep, and hot in
Scotland. The very motto of the clan Campbell is
"Never Forget." And when it came to the feud between the
MacDonalds and the Campbells, the chiefs of the Campbells
seem, at least at first glance, to have remembered old
enmities while making the decisions that led up to the
massacre at Glencoe.

Like the Campbells' problems with the MacGregors, the
MacDonald—Campbell feud went straight back to the first
Scottish War of Independence, when the MacDonalds had
chosen the losing side in fighting against Robert the Bruce.
In subsequent wars and skirmishes throughout the centuries

since, the MacDonalds had demonstrated an almost uncanny knack for backing the wrong horse, while the Campbells had been either lucky, treacherous, or politically very skillful—depending on who you choose to ask. That question is still debated.

In the wake of two rapid-fire Argyll executions following the restoration of the crown to Charles II and—briefly—to his brother James thereafter, though, the Campbells found themselves in dire political straights. With his father's head on a Scottish pike, the son of the ninth Earl of Argyll had worked hard, trying to wiggle back into James II's good graces. That hadn't gone so well, but since James wasn't on the throne very long, it hadn't been an insurmountable obstacle. With Mary and William of Orange firmly seated on a united British throne, he had better luck.

By supporting the new Dutch king against James Stuart, the tenth Earl of Argyll earned back his father's land and titles. Going one better, in 1689, he mustered the first standing infantry regiment in Scotland on William's behalf—Argyll's Regiment of Foot—which was used to beat down Jacobite rebellion in the Highlands. This, in turn, contributed to earning him the shiny new title of Duke of Argyll in 1701.

Soon enough, he had a seat on the king's Privy Council, and he became the king's chief Scottish advisor.

Peace in the Highlands, and Scotland in general, was critical for William of Orange. Links between the MacDonalds of Scotland and branches of the family in Ireland, not to mention other Scots families that had settled in Scotland during the Ulster Plantations, often bled trouble from one country to another. And William couldn't afford to be putting down uprisings in either country, because he needed soldiers to fight for him in Europe, where the Nine Years' War (not the Tyrone Rebellion of the same name that was fought in Ireland against Elizabeth I, but a brand new European version) was underway.

But the Highlands were restive. The MacDonalds, along with the Grahams under Bonnie Dundee, the Camerons under Lochiel, and a host of other Highland families like the MacGregors, had risen with the Jacobites against William and Mary for James Stuart. They hadn't given up when Dundee was killed at Killiecrankie, and they continued fighting even after James' last hopes were soundly defeated in the Irish battle that saw nearly 8,000 Jacobites dead in Aughrim. Part of the problem was that the Presbyterians and former Covenanters were now firmly in power in Parliament and had begun to pay out old scores, not only against Catholics but also against anyone who came down on the side of the Church of England in terms of religious practice and structure. This encompassed many of the clans.

Hard-pressed to pacify the Highlands by force, something that had never really worked well in the entire history of Scotland, William tried to bring the clans back to the fold by offering a pardon. This was backed by cold hard cash to anyone who swore him an oath of allegiance. Because the alternative was a series of punitive reprisals, the clans reluctantly gave at least the appearance of agreement. But a secret amendment reportedly supported by most of the chiefs canceled the oath in the event of a new Jacobite invasion, making it basically worthless.

That amendment, when its existence was leaked, did not make William happy. (Yes, they had leaks even back then. Politics doesn't change much through the centuries.)

The problem was placed squarely at the feet of the MacDonald chief, but it was a symptom of the deep political and financial infighting among the Highland chiefs. Partly to disguise the nature of that infighting, partly because it was true, and partly because it was guaranteed to receive a favorable reception in some quarters, this was put down to religion and general lawlessness.

Again, William himself was not anti-Catholic per se. More of an opportunist. And though it's clear that the rising religious intolerance in Scotland upset and often infuriated him, he didn't seem to have done anything to stamp it out. Long story short, because it was critical for William to calm the Highlands, he further made a critical mistake in choosing the individual to whom he entrusted the delicate negotiations, namely the Earl of Breadelbane.

Breadelbane, the Campbell of Glenlyon, having gotten his hands on the £12,000 to £15,000—an enormous sum back then—with which to pay all the Highland clans in exchange for peace, seems to have been reluctant to let it slip between his fingers. His close relative, the Earl of Argyll, similarly seems to have been inclined to take an extra bit for himself. The negotiations, therefore, involved also the question of how much each clan would get, relative to other clans, and whether the clans who owed money to Argyll should get the money at all before their entire debt to Argyll had been paid. To this was added the demands Breadelbane himself placed on the MacDonald of Glencoe, from whom he demanded reparations for years of cattle rustling. Faced with the prospect of not getting anything out of the settlement for himself, MacDonald wasn't terribly inclined to cooperate, and since he was well respected by the other chiefs, he managed to derail the negotiations with Breadelbane over and over again.

After a long, hard slog against French and Jacobite forces in Ireland, William had finally managed to quell the rebellion there. The Treaty of Limerick had been newly signed in October, and William wanted nothing to renew hostilities.

To keep things from dragging on in the Highlands, the authorities in Edinburgh did a bit of an end run and announced that any clan who swore an oath of loyalty to William by January 1, 1692 would receive a pardon. Any clan that didn't, well, they would have cause to regret it. And because preparations for war were clearly underway on the part of the government, the clans took the threat quite seriously.

Out of money themselves and out of hope for receiving additional funds from the exiled King James for mounting a continuing rebellion on his behalf themselves, the clans felt they had no choice except to accept the peace. That said, they wanted to protect themselves by first getting explicit permission from James to take the oath. After all, they were still hoping against hope for a new Jacobite invasion force, and if that did happen, the last thing they wanted was to end up with James accusing them of treason—that would have meant being on the losing side either way if war broke out again.

James' permission to get themselves pardoned was late arriving, and what with one thing or another, none of the chiefs wanted to be the first to sign. They sent their clansmen and vassals off to get themselves pardoned, but they danced around each other, continued posturing, and otherwise generally delayed.

MacDonald of Glencoe left it until the last second to set off. He and a number of his vassals arrived at Fort William on the 30th of December, only to discover that there was no magistrate there authorized to accept the oath. Whether he'd been told that location deliberately, or whether it was an accident, remains in dispute. But unable to help them, the governor at Fort William sent them on to Sir Colin Campbell in Inverary, with a letter explaining that the chief had, in fact, arrived before the deadline so everything was all right. Campbell gave the MacDonalds the oath on the 6th of January. Other clan chiefs took it even later. The MacDonalds went home to Glencoe thinking all was well.

It wasn't. On behalf of William and with his blessing, the John Dalrymple, Secretary of State and Maste of Stair, had already issued orders for the military commander of Scotland to immediately seize the opportunity to kill the members—and destroy the property—of particular clans if they failed to sign the oath. These clans included the MacDonalds and Camerons because their chiefs were "papists," along with several others who were particularly targeted for being problematic. News that the MacDonalds of Glencoe hadn't signed the oath on time was met with delight by Argyll and Breadelbane, but particularly by John Dalrymple, for whom pacifying the Highlands and getting rid of the "thieving" clans had become almost a mania.

> "Your troops will destroy entirely the country of Lochaber, Lochiel's lands, Keppoch's, Glengarry's and Glencoe's," he wrote. ". . . I hope the soldiers will not trouble the government with prisoners."

Within weeks, the Earl of Argyll's Regiment of Foot was sent out to the MacDonald country in Glencoe under the command of Captain Robert Campbell with orders demanding "free quarter," a custom by which, in place of taxes, a landowner was required to provide hospitality for troops or militia in service to the government. The troops stayed for two weeks on apparently good terms with their hosts, being fed, housed, given entertainment.

In short, receiving hospitality from the clan MacDonald.

This question of hospitality is important. Under Highland custom, you didn't refuse to give hospitality when it was requested of you. Nor did you betray hospitality when it was given.

Except that's exactly what the Argyll Regiment under Captain Robert Campbell did—on orders from John Dalrymple, the Highlander-loathing zealot.

> Sir,
>
> You are hereby ordered to fall upon the rebels, the M'Donalds, of Glencoe and putt all to the sword under seventy. You are to have special care that the old fox and his sons doe upon no account escape your hands. You are to secure all the avenues, that no man may escape. This you are to putt in execution at five o'clock in the morning

precisely, and by that time, or very shortly after it, I'll strive to be att you with a stronger party. If I doe not come to you att five, you are not to tarry for me, but to fall on. This is by the king's special command, for the good of the country, that these miscreants be cutt off root and branch. See that this be putt in execution without feud or favour, else you may expect to be treated as not true to the king's government, nor a man fitt to carry a commission in the king's service. Expecting you will not faill in the fulfilling hereof as you love yourself, I subscribe these with my hand.

Master of the Stair

(John Dalrymple)

On the 13th of February, at five o'clock in the morning, the members of the Argyll Regiment got out of their beds and began to slaughter their hosts. Additional troops from the regiment moved in to cut off escape from both the north and south, sealing the MacDonald's inside the glen.

Fortunately, again whether by accident or minor

rebellion is debatable, these additional men arrived hours after they were meant to, otherwise the ensuing massacre would have been much worse.

Massacre, you ask?

Oh, absolutely.

In all, the Argyll troops killed thirty-eight MacDonald men outright that morning in a snowstorm. They then proceeded to take away all the livestock and set fire to all the houses throughout the glen. To the death toll from the initial slaughter, one must, therefore, add an additional forty women and children who froze or starved to death when their food and shelter were destroyed or stolen. A total of seventy-eight people, with many more gravely wounded. The brutality was singular. A twelve-year-old boy clinging to a soldier's leg begging for mercy was shot. The MacDonald chief's wife was stripped of her clothes and jewelry, and when a ring wouldn't come easily away, a soldier bit her finger off.

And had the troops managed to fully seal the glen as originally planned, the death toll could have been much worse. Honestly, according to the orders, it could have been much worse given that all under seventy were meant to be killed.

As for the soldiers of Argyll's Foot themselves? While history has since taken the position that receiving an order does not provide a defense when it comes to atrocities, back then it was much harder to refuse an order than it is today—there simply wasn't anywhere a man could go after that, and reprisals from those who had given the order could be harsh against both the man and his family. The threat of reprisal against Captain Campbell is right there in the letter.

It's a complicated situation, and still one that is deeply charged. To this day, there are places in Scotland that have "No Campbells" signs, and the clan has had to bear the aftermath of Glencoe through the centuries. This isn't entirely fair. Though other hands carried out the massacre, it was a mainly a device of two greedy men and a zealot. Ultimately, the buck stops at William, and he wasn't concerned. Even as the word of the massacre slowly got out, within the British realms little happened. It wasn't until the news of the brutality was leaked overseas in Europe that anger against William began to mount.

And that, in turn, fanned the fervor of the Jacobite rebellion. Bonnie Prince Charlie even had pamphlets about the massacre printed and distributed in 1745 to help with his recruiting effort.

Not every Campbell involved in this incident or any other is bad. Not every Campbell is blameless. Not every MacDonald (or MacGregor or . . . and so on ad infinitum) is either bad or good. There had been many massacres and brutal acts among the Highland clans up to then, and there were a few more yet to come. The level of brutality that was soon to hit the Highlands on behalf of the Crown was going to be far, far worse in many ways. But for many of the men in the Argyll Regiment, remorse started to set in. Breadalbane himself was said to be a changed man, haunted by the events.

But the massacre of Glencoe seems to have left not only a wound on Scottish history, but on the landscape of Glencoe itself.

I can personally attest to that. Walking in the glen is an eerie experience. The mist weeps down the braes and collects in gullies, and there's a chill in the air that invades your bones even in the balm of summer.

In some ways, it changed the political climate as well. The aftermath slowly turned from quiet whispers of outrage into a swelling roar.

The Loss of Scotland

"We will drain our dearest veins,
But they shall be free."

ROBERT BURNS

W ITH THE DEFEAT OF Jacobite forces in Ireland and
the loss of Highland support, King James had
temporarily given up efforts to regain his throne through
military strength. But that didn't mean he or his supporters
were entirely giving up. In 1691, the Williamite defeat of the
Irish had sent most of the Irish soldiers—the Wild Geese—
flying from Ireland with their families.

In May of 1692, the king of France, with James firmly on
his side—or vice versa, depending on how you looked at it—
sailed an armada of forty-four ships of the line from France,
carrying a mixed army of French troops, Irish "Wild Geese,"
and assorted English Jacobite supporters to restore James to
the throne of England. Under the command of the Comte

de Tourville, they hoped to reach England before the Dutch and English ships had taken to the water after the long winter, but a series of blunders and misconceptions resulted in them facing, instead, a combined Anglo-Dutch force of eight-two ships. Still, they fought well under overwhelming odds, and, with many ships damaged on both sides, Tourville slipped away from the battle in a combination of physical fog and the fog of war.

The French scattered, Louis XIV gave up on attempting naval superiority and concentrated instead on impeding English trade and on winning the ground war in Europe.

His own hopes dashed and a fresh military campaign seemingly out of the question, James concentrated on brewing a different type of campaign. Any number of plots were hatched, including assassination plots against William himself.

That didn't end well for the Jacobites. In fact, following the death of Queen Mary II from smallpox in 1694, whisperings about the legitimacy of a continued crown for her husband, William, were quelled by an assassination attempt in 1696 where William was saved by what was seen as "divine providence."

On such small things hang the fate of kings.

The Scottish Jacobites weren't quiet, either. They were simply keeping their heads down brewing fresh new plots. And from their perspective, they had reason.

Queen Mary had died childless, and her sister, Princess Anne—James' youngest daughter and next in line to the throne—had no surviving children, either, despite seventeen pregnancies. (Poor Anne!)

In 1702, the question of who would inherit the throne was all just theory. But then William, riding a feisty horse confiscated from a Jacobite rebel, took a fall and broke his collarbone. Pneumonia ensued, and he died.

Had King James lived to see this, he might have believed it was divine intervention sending a message that the tide had finally turned and God was actually Team James. The exiled king had died just months earlier, though, of a brain hemorrhage at his home in France.

And now Scotland was about to be dealt yet another blow.

King James had written out long and detailed instructions to his son, James Francis Edward Stuart, who came to be called the "Old Pretender" for the time when he finally regained his crown. Surely on the death of William the world would finally tilt back on its axis and the farce of the

Jacobite exile would come to an end? William and Mary didn't have any living heirs, after all.

But no. The throne went to Mary's sister—King James' remaining daughter—Anne. Even worse, though Queen Anne was at least a Stuart, she had no children either, so now the obvious (Protestant) candidates for succession ended. Rather than accept the idea of a Catholic monarch in the event something happened to Anne, the English Parliament had adopted the Act of Settlement in 1701, which barred any of Anne's Catholic relatives from the throne and gave the English crown (along with that of Scotland and Ireland) to a very distant relation in German Hanover.

In Scotland, this wasn't particularly popular. Ireland had long since lost its independence and Wales had become part of England, but Scotland had until this point managed to keep its own laws and parliament—and the Scots wanted the right to choose their own ruler, too, not have some upstart appointed for them. They'd already been through that once.

Anne called for a joint commission to try to reach a compromise, but after four months of discussions, they gave up in 1703 and all went home. The Scots passed an Act of Security that allowed them to officially pick Anne's successor for the Scottish throne from among the Protestant descendants of the royal Scottish line. The Act further stipulated that this ruler would *not* be the same person as the English ruler—not unless the English first agreed to give Scotland freedom of trade.

Anne had long since decided that she wanted England and Scotland to come closer together in terms of government, not further apart. Still, she signed the Scottish Act when the Scots threatened to refuse to support military action. In retaliation, England issued the Alien Act of 1705, taking away the rights of Scottish citizens. To prevent huge problems, Scotland could give up the Security Act. The Scottish Parliament chose plan B instead, and voted to become part of a united Britain—no longer a separate nation. This was confirmed by both the English and Scottish Parliaments in 1707, and Great Britain was formed.

Opposition ensued on both sides of the border—and also across the English Channel in France.

Living in exile in France, James Francis Stuart managed to cajole the French king into giving him an invasion fleet of thirty ships in 1708 that sailed out of Dunkirk with 6,000 French troops on board. James—having drunk the Kool-Aid sold to him by people trying to tell him what he wanted to hear—had bought into the idea that most of Britain would be waiting to welcome him home with banners waving, and that even the British navy would stand down and refuse to fight. Having grown up in an environment where he and his family lived on charity and were used as pawns in the power plays of the king of France while remaining at the French King's mercy, he and his father had simultaneously become the pipe-dream of lost nations, nations who—rightly or wrongly—saw in them the hope of salvation, dignity, prosperity, and duty.

Yes, duty. Jacobites truly believed in the idea that kings were accountable only to God, and that God, in turn, required obedience to kings. In their view, King James had been removed from his legal and rightful monarchy by an *illegal* Convention Parliament, so, therefore, they had a duty to resist such removal. There were Catholic Jacobites, certainly. The Stuarts themselves were Catholics, and King James' Declaration of Indulgence in 1687 had promised religious freedom to all denominations. They were Unionists, though, in favor of a single British monarchy and government. The Scottish Jacobites were, by this point, mostly Protestants who weren't about to accept a foreign king when they saw the rightful Scottish king as the true sovereign of England and Ireland as well. They wanted to dissolve the Union and have Scotland be its own nation once again. And the mostly Catholic Irish? King James had promised the Irish Parliament the right to eventually govern themselves. Like the Scots, therefore, they were fighting as much if not more for their freedom as for a man they truly saw as king.

James Francis, having been brought up with all this, was a dreamer. Wistful, romantic, a little spoiled. Utterly lacking in moral courage, or perhaps to some extent he feared to disappoint his supporters. It must have been hard to have so many hopes resting on his head when he knew that he was not at all the type of a leader who could charge decisively into battle and command. And something about him, whether it was the dream itself or the recognition that he wanted desperately to believe in that dream, did manage to buy him some personal support.

This was the problem in 1708. He believed what people told him, and perhaps because he so much wanted to believe it, people also told him what he wanted to hear.

He pictured himself returning triumphantly to Britain, greeted by uprisings in Scotland as well as England. He imagined the navy—if it even materialized—raising his flag when they saw him coming. Instead, the British admiralty was waiting at the Firth of Forth, and the French turned tail and headed home, despite James' tearful entreaties to the contrary.

Queen Anne died in 1714, and the 1701 Act of Succession skipped straight over more than fifty Catholic heirs with closer claims—not to mention deeper connections to the country they were about to rule. The crown of Great Britain went to Anne's German second cousin George Ludwig.

That was another great tipping point for the Jacobites. They were joined by freshly deposed rivals to the new British political establishment, and everyone called for a military campaign. James wrote to the pope pleading for support in helping him to save his country and the church.

The Earl of Mar sailed to Scotland and, together with 600 soldiers, raised James' standard as a call to war. By October of 1714, the Earl of Mar had 20,000 men, and with the exception of Stirling Castle, he'd taken all of Scotland north of the Firth of Forth.

Opposing him was the Duke of Argyll—the son of the man who'd been involved in the Glencoe massacre. And this Duke was a different sort of man altogether. He had years of military experience fighting actual war in Europe as opposed to concentrating on political infighting. He understood battlefield tactics and strategy. By 1710, he was the general in charge of all British forces in Spain, and in 1712 he returned to Scotland as commander-in-chief. He'd been supportive of the plan to give the throne to the Hanovarian king all along, so there was no question of his loyalty.

The two armies clashed in the Battle of Sherifmuir on November 13, 1715, and though the Jacobite forces under the Earl of Mar outnumbered Argyll's army four to one by the end of the battle, for once the Highlanders and Jacobites did not prevail. Mar's men failed to press home their advantage, and Argyll's forces retreated.

Sheriffmuir ended in a draw, but simultaneous battles at Inverness and Preston resulted in Jacobite losses. The Jacobite forces held on. On the 22nd of December, James finally landed in Scotland, but he was physically ill— something that only got worse with the deep cold of the Scottish Highlands. By then the Jacobite forces had been whittled down to less than 5,000 men while Argyll's forces were strengthened by more men and heavy artillery. James briefly tried to hold court at Scone Palace in Perth, but as Argyll's army approached he was forced to concede defeat. Bursting into tears, he was whisked off to France once again.

This time, though, he was no longer welcome at the court of the French king, who had cut a deal with the British in the meantime. James took refuge in Avignon, which, at the time, was the territory of the pope. Subsequent Popes offered him sanctuary in Rome, along with a handsome stipend. His father had died living quite austerely, but James Francis was able to set up a glittering Jacobite court that, a bit in the style of Elizabeth I, helped to keep the propaganda machine nicely rolling along. Even so, he suffered from depression.

In Britain, meanwhile, the price for his supporters was a heavy one. In England, men had already been arrested for treason both before and after the conflicts in Scotland. To this number, the names of all those who had participated in the Scottish Risings were added.

Treasonous MacGregors

*"Him the tribes of Lonach and the
widely spread Clan of MacGregor
accompanied as their leader."*

JAMES PHILLIP
"THE GRAMEID"

T HE BRITISH PRISONS WERE full of Jacobites in 1716. So
many that the government had to draw lots to decide
who would face trial. But many managed to remain at large.
In Scotland, the old familiar question came up again: how to
pacify the Highland clans?

And here's where we come back to the MacGregors—
and the Dukes of Argyll and Montrose.

From Dublin in 1689, James had given the Laird of
MacGregor, chief of the clan MacGregor, a commission as
colonel of a regiment in Scotland, with the power to raise his
own officers and men. Gregor MacGregor, the fifteenth

chief, then made Donald Glas MacGregor, the father of Robert Roy MacGregor, the lieutenant colonel of the regiment, and Rob and his father raised men for the Battle of Killicrankie.

Following that battle, Donald had been arrested and spent two years in prison before returning home a broken man.

Rob, in his absence, had been busy. He'd built up a legitimate business driving cattle, but he'd coupled that with a flair for blackmail—or the seventeenth-century equivalent of a protection scheme—in which he coaxed (mostly) Lowland farmers to pay him to "watch" their cattle and keep them from getting stolen. The farmers who didn't pay found their cattle whisked away—and Rob and his cohorts miraculously ended up with a correspondingly greater number of cattle to take to market. Rob was, by many accounts, assisted in this scheme by the Duke of Montrose, the descendant of the enemy of the erstwhile Earls of Argyll, who (it's alleged) received a share of some of Rob Roy's illegal proceeds.

Montrose apparently hadn't heard the term "honor among thieves," though. In 1711, when Rob had needed money to expand his cattle business, he had turned to

Montrose for a loan, but the enormous sum of money was then stolen by an employee of Rob's, and Montrose took the opportunity to seize Rob's land and cattle and have Rob outlawed.

From that time until the Rising of 1715, there had been an ongoing feud with Montrose, and Rob had turned to his mother's relative, the Duke of Argyll, for help and protection. And although there had never been love lost between the Argyll family of Campbells and the MacGregors, the family history of animosity (and debt) between the Duke of Argyll and the Duke of Montrose ran deeper. It became a case of the enemy-of-my-enemy-is-my-friend.

From a rented property on Argyll's land in Glen Dochart, Rob Roy waged a systematic campaign of retribution against the Duke of Montrose, stealing his cattle and making him ridiculous through a host of clever ruses. Think Robin Hood and the Sheriff of Nottingham—that's not too far off, and truthfully, perhaps that legend inspired some pieces of the novel. Anyway, Rob was able to pull all this off with relative (pardon the pun) impunity because of Argyll's protection.

For the sake of that protection and Argyll's government

allegiances, Rob stayed out of the major battles in the 1715 Jacobite Rising. That didn't help him. He was accused of treason along with the other Jacobites in 1716, and Montrose made sure that he wasn't overlooked. With his property forfeit once more, Montrose—again—also took full advantage financially.

The feud between them escalated once again. This time, Rob wasn't playing around anymore. He straight up kidnapped Graham of Killearn, Montrose's factor—the man who managed the duke's business and the money he was owed. Graham, in captivity, wrote to Montrose on Rob's orders, letting Montrose know that he was "so fortunate at present as to be his [Rob's] prisoner" and asking Montrose (doubtless on Rob's instructions) to forgive Rob all sums that Rob owed. In addition, he advised Montrose to pay Rob an enormous sum of money in penalties and restitution.

Montrose complained to the Crown instead, not only about the kidnapping of his factor, but simultaneously providing a description of all of Rob's alleged involvement in the 1715 Jacobite Rising. This all then came into play in 1717, when the rest of the Highland clans—with a few specific exceptions—were pardoned by King George. Care to guess who was named as an exception? You guessed it.

Robert Roy MacGregor. And the entire MacGregor clan.

Once again, though, the Duke of Argyll managed to step in and help stave off the worst of the punishment for Rob, and with the help of a lot of sympathetic Highlanders, Rob managed to remain in the Highlands instead of having to leave the country. Montrose briefly captured him, but he escaped, and though he was hunted by a wide variety of troops, including General Carpenter, he managed to evade them, too. At least for a number of years.

In 1719, Rob took part in yet another failed uprising, and then in 1722, his luck finally ran out. Captured, he was held prisoner for five years. While incarcerated, he converted to Catholicism. And in 1723, the infamous—and anonymous, although it's commonly attributed to Daniel Defoe—novel was published about his exploits and turned him into an overnight sensation throughout much of Britain.

In 1727, Rob was due to be transported to America in one of the prisoner "plantation" schemes, but King George I, having heard of—and possibly even read—the novel, issued a pardon and granted Rob his freedom. Rob died peacefully in the Balquhidder glen in 1734, and so he missed the final chapters of the Jacobite rebellions—and the final punishment and tragedy that was to befall the Highlands in their wake.

Long March to Culloden

"And a whisper awoke on the wilderness, sighing,
Like the voice of the heroes who battled in vain,
"Not for Tearlach alone the red claymore was plying,
But to bring back the old life that comes not again."

ANDREW LANG
"CULLODEN"

THE JACOBITE CAUSE HAD lost considerably when the long Nine Years' War in Europe finally ended in 1713. The Treaty of Utrecht—and the years of continental conflict leading up to it—had changed the balance of power in Europe. The British navy was now the biggest in the world, and the previous superpowers—France, Spain, and the Dutch—were all economically fragile and depleted. Unable to afford additional conflict, France signed the Anglo-French treaty in 1716, which was the reason why, in exchange for a fragile peace, Louis had booted James and his Jacobites out of France.

Next to James Francis himself, Spain had arguably come out the biggest loser in the war, despite the fact that the grandson of the king of France ended up on the Spanish throne. Not only had Spain lost the southern Netherlands, Savoy, Menorca, Gibraltar, and parts of Italy, they'd also had to give British merchants the right to trade in South America, which up until then had been Spain's own personal gold mine and playground.

For a few years, Phillip quietly schemed about how to rebuild the Spanish empire. He tried to recoup some control of the Mediterranean in 1718 with troops in Sardinia and Sicily, but the English, Dutch, and French allied with the Holy Roman Empire against him. So, by 1719, he was starting to think that helping a suitably grateful James Stuart plant himself on the British throne might not be such a bad idea. Or, as an alternative plan, that stirring up the possibility of a Jacobite invasion might occupy the British fleet long enough for his own navy to make some further inroads in the Mediterranean.

Long story short, while the idea of 5,000 or more Spanish troops and a Spanish fleet was bandied about, and there was brief involvement from the Swedish king, the success of an invasion force that size actually making a successful crossing and landing was never very high. Ultimately, only 300 Spanish troops managed to navigate through the weather. They were met in the Western Isles by a group of Jacobite exiles, including the ever-loyal Cameron of Lochiel, Lord George Murray, the Earl of Seaforth, the Earl Marischal, and the Marquess of Tullibardine, along with a number of Irish officers. Dismay ensued when they found that the promised 5,000 Spanish forces weren't there and likely weren't coming.

Now came the question of what to do. If they waited in the hope of Spanish assistance, the government garrison at Inverness was bound to discover them and they'd lose any element of surprise. But the Jacobites had never lacked courage or daring.

On April 13, 1719, they went ahead alone and landed at Eilean Donan, the small island where Loch Duich, Loch Long, and Loch Alsh come together in the western Highlands. They set up the Jacobite headquarters at the Mackenzie stronghold there, where legend had it that Robert the Bruce himself had already taken refuge during the Wars of Scottish Independence. With opinions split about whether to stay or go when the Spanish still hadn't arrived, the Earl

Marischal settled the matter by sending away the frigates that had brought them over. In effect, this stranded them all on the island with the 300 Spanish troops and 2,000 Spanish guns they had brought with them to arm the fresh rising of the Highland clans they expected to come to James' standard.

They were a long way from needing that many guns. The Clan Mackenzie rose to meet them, along the with Clan MacRae and the Clan MacGregor, including Rob Roy himself and some others. Still, all told, it was under a thousand men. Deciding they couldn't wait any longer, Seaforth, Lochiel, and Murray left a small garrison at Eilean Donan and led their forces south to capture the garrison at Inverness and stir up as much additional support as they could muster.

But the government wasn't idle while this was happening. Five ships soon slipped in around Eilean Donan and bombarded the castle walls. Then they disembarked troops, captured the castle relatively easily, and sailed the Spanish prisoners off to Edinburgh, leaving the Jacobites with no ready refuge to which they could return.

The Jacobite ground force made it about twelve miles to Glen Shiel, a long valley flanked by tall ridges—a beautiful spot with strong natural fortifications. But they were met there by a government force of 850 infantry, 120 mounted cavalry troops, and—most importantly—four mobile mortar batteries, something that hadn't yet been used extensively in infantry warfare. The high angle trajectories of these heavier artillery weapons, together with their explosive power, gave them an advantage over traditional field guns in the mountainous and rocky Highland terrain.

The numbers on the Jacobite side and the government forces, if you discounted the advantage of the mortars and the mounted dragoons, were fairly even. The Jacobite positions were also stronger in terms of terrain and fortification. But from the beginning, the artillery made all the difference. The government forces under General Joseph Wightman, who had already fought beside Argyll at Sheriffmuir and knew Highlander tactics well, first shelled Lord Murray's men heavily before advancing against them and breaking the Jacobite right wing. They then concentrated firepower and men on the Jacobite left, but simultaneously shelled the main Jacobite center and kept the Spanish troops pinned down.

Within three hours, the Spanish troops surrendered. The surviving Jacobite forces—those who weren't too heavily wounded—slipped away in the fog that habitually clung to the hillsides of Glen Shiel and much of the Highlands.

The Rising of 1719 was broken, and its defeated and demoralized leaders mostly returned to France or Prussia to live in exile.

This was by no means the end of the Jacobite movement, though. The Hanovarian King George was deeply unpopular, together with the Whig government that had—overreachingly, many believed—brought him into power by deciding that Parliament had the right to decide the succession instead of relying on hereditary rights. To complicate matters, the king's own son hated his father and opposed him personally and politically at every turn.

This was compounded by a wave of speculation in the South Sea Company—think of it a bit like tech stock bubble minus the tech—that embroiled vast sums of the national debt and resulted in a massive crash that ruined much of the British aristocracy. The resulting financial crisis was followed by a reshuffling of power surrounding George. By 1722, Sir Robert Walpole had emerged as the de facto first Prime Minister of Great Britain. (He's acknowledged as the first, though he didn't technically hold that title.) George exercised less and less leadership over anything but foreign affairs after that, and through his inaction and that of his son, the power of the Crown gradually diminished while the power of the prime minister continued growing.

History hasn't done the Georges any favors. At least George I. Because the first George was fifty by the time he became king, he never cultivated much of a relationship with his subjects. His command of English wasn't originally great, though he had learned it well by the time he died. He was, moreover, reserved and awkward with those he didn't know, even more than Queen Anne had been, and he felt the disdain of the English people who commonly laughed at him or mocked him.

George II, in contrast, courted popularity and lapped up the interest of his English subjects from the moment of his arrival in England as a young prince of Wales. He caused such a stir, in contrast to his father, that George I was apparently jealous of his son. And when a scuffle occurred over a baptism custom, the father had the son and his wife banned from the palace—but kept his grandchildren with him at his own court. The prince and princess of Wales had to beg permission to visit their own children, and reportedly even tried sneaking in on one occasion.

In a turn of irony, George II's own son hated him just as much as George had in turn hated his own father. To avoid having George at the birth of his child, the prince whisked his wife out of the palace while she was in labor, with the result that the two were banned from court much as George himself had been.

By this time, the second of the Hanovarian Georges was no more popular than his father had been. And Tories, the mostly Church of England Protestant disaffected leaders in Parliament who had lost more and more power to the Whigs and now seemed destined to never get it back, sided increasingly with the Jacobites. Their numbers gave James Francis and his son Charles a bit of hope that was destined to be false.

On the surface of it, the Jacobite cause seemed to have support. Perhaps even enough support to mount a fresh military campaign to retake the throne.

In reality, the interests of the Jacobite factions were often in conflict among three different religions, and the supporters of each of these all felt their own should take precedence. There were also supporters of three different nations, each in conflict about how much independence and sovereignty their own country and the others deserved. In addition, lack of support for the Hanovarian king was easily confused with Stuart support—but they were not one and the same. The nature of Jacobite support, true support, was as hard to grasp as Highland fog, and when pushed too hard from any direction, it had a tendency to drift away.

In truth, Jacobitism had little to do with personal support for King James, his son the "Old Pretender" or "Old Cavalier," or even for his grandson "Bonnie" Prince Charlie. It was a struggle for a cause, an opposition to a loss of control, a grand idea nursed by men who longed for something grander than reality. Had there been stronger or shrewder men, more united men, at the heart of this struggle, it might have ended differently, but the brave and deeply honorable supporters who surrounded the royals were often themselves at odds.

This was no different in 1744 than it had been in 1715.

With Robert Walpole ousted as prime minister and a fresh political betrayal of the conservative Tories (whose beginnings were pro-Jacobite) by the Whig (anti-absolute monarchy, anti-Jacobite, and pro-Presbyterian) majority in Parliament, the environment in England was rife with disaffected politicians. A new war was brewing again between France and Britain as well. Louis XV, the French king—who'd been getting requests from Jacobites for military intervention all along—decided perhaps the time was right to listen. He sent an envoy to Scotland to scout out possible Jacobite support, and having gotten a favorable report, he notified his uncle in Spain that he was going to lend James Francis troops and attempt an invasion across the English Channel. What he didn't intend to do, however, was risk bringing Charles Edward Stuart to Paris until after the war was won.

He failed to mention that to Charles or James.

While Louis gathered 12,000 men and transports at Dunkirk and planned to use his navy to draw off British ships to give the troop transports time to cross the Channel, Charles Edward Stuart undertook a fraught secret journey to France to join them.

But the idea of an invasion had already been leaked. The plan fell apart, and war between France and Britain was declared. Fighting openly on the European continent, Louis was no longer as interested in sending his forces to Scotland—if he ever truly had been.

This rankled both James and his son. In anticipation of another push to retake the throne of Britain, Charles—the "Bonnie" prince or the "Young Pretender," had been trained for the military campaign to take back the Stuart throne his entire life. And he was itching to get started.

If the Jacobite cause was cobbled together from many different dreams, Bonnie Prince Charlie was the perfect ribbon on which to hang them. From the outset—despite Hanovarian propaganda—he was handsome, engaging, and lively. Full of energy and kindness as a child, he charmed everyone who came in contact with him. And this included many people. The Jacobite court in Rome became a popular tourist destination. His father gave away "peerages" for favors. Want to be an English lord? Get your titles here. Need help while you're abroad? Stop by. We have the best doctors to attend you, and we'll do our best in every respect.

To win support, James Francis made his court into a living dream of glittering court life, a stark contrast to the regimented pomp, sobriety, and serious lack of fun that was the Hanovarian court in London.

Beneath the glamour, though, there was trouble brewing. James Francis often argued with Charles' mother, the nervous and somewhat volatile Clementina, Princess of Poland. James Francis was suffering more and more from alternating fits of depression and manic optimism.

As if he realized how many hopes were draped around his slim shoulders, Charles, the young prince, seemed from an early age to grasp that he needed to deserve those hopes. A letter from the Duke of Liria suggests he was quite exceptional at the age of six and a half:

> "Not only could he read fluently, he could ride, fire a gun; and more surprisingly still, I have seen him take a cross-bow and kill birds on the roof and split a rolling ball with a bolt ten times in succession. He speaks English, French, and Italian perfectly and altogether is the most perfect Prince I have ever met in my life."

As one can imagine, though, brought up in this environment, the child who tries so hard to please can also end up feeling the pressure. Charles could be moody and temperamental as well. But much of the modern view of Charles—and even the historical writing about him—was based on slanted information. Already as a young man, he was both vilified and glorified depending on which side someone chose to take.

First, there was the subject of his education. Much to the horror of Charles' mother, who also had a personal distaste for the man, James Francis chose James Murray to play a significant role in the prince's education—and Murray was an Episcopalian. Clementina duly reported this to the pope, who was paying for the entire court and on whose charity the Stuarts depended. Naturally, the pope was not best pleased. Why had James done this? There was, perhaps, some thought even then that Charles would need a balanced perspective, if he were ever to be king in truth, some way in which to relate to the bulk of his potential subjects— especially in Scotland and England—who were mostly not, by this time, Roman Catholic. In fact, Charles secretly converted to the Church of England later in life—after the disaster at Culloden—hoping for this same thing.

At the time, though, the argument about Charles' education escalated—and the marriage of his parents deteriorated. After the birth of his brother Henry Benedict, Clementina took herself off to a convent in a huff, and with the further objection from the king of Spain to having Charles educated by someone other than a Catholic, the young Charles was called before the pope himself and grilled on all things a good Catholic should know in an attempt to make certain he wasn't being taught any heresies. (There'd been all sorts of accusations made about Murray's teachings.)

No wonder Charles grew resentful and frustrated. Murray also seems to have been a stern taskmaster. At the age of thirteen, Charles reportedly kicked the man and threatened to kill him if he didn't stop chastising him. What exactly Murray was doing to him isn't clear—but with both his mother and the pope himself having accused Murray of being evil, it might not be too much of a stretch to imagine that Charles wasn't willing to accept everything he said or did without question. And interestingly, Charles had an excellent relationship with his other tutor, an Irish Protestant who had converted to Catholicism, that lasted for many years. (That same tutor later became one of Charles' chief advisors during the Jacobite Rising of 1745.)

All of this educational controversy, meanwhile, provided rich fodder to anyone who opposed the Jacobite cause.

About this same time, the Hanovarians in London had caught wind of Charles as a possible threat to the Crown. He was, after all, what neither of the king Georges—nor even King James and James Francis had ever been: a handsome, charismatic leader and someone who could potentially inspire the love and devotion of his followers. His father made the most of this, dressing him in Highland dress and jewels as he was presented at the various courts of Europe.

Added to the "dream" that was the Jacobite cause, this PR campaign, coupled with Charles' own personal attributes, came to be seen as a serious threat. The Hanovarians and their supporters, therefore, did everything they could to counter it. Rumors were spread about Charles weaknesses. His boorishness. His conceit. His stupidity. His illiteracy.

This was easily picked up after the tide of historical interpretation shifted in the wake of the disaster at Culloden, when Charlie went from being the dashing hero, the embodiment of hope, to being a whipping boy, the idiot prince who cost the Jacobites everything.

Most of this was British—Hanovarian—propaganda. And it was sold wholesale to the Scots over the past quarter of a millennium. It doesn't matter how many historians dispute it, that the archeology bears out what many modern historians argue, or what the primary sources from the immediate aftermath of Culloden say. Certain ideas caught on and proved persistent, and certain people—the young prince first and foremost—were vilified. That the viewpoint was intentional to safeguard the union and prevent another uprising, to finally stomp out Scottish nationalism, in effect, seems too often still to be overlooked.

But history is never a set of hard facts—because not all the facts come down to us. Nor are *all* the facts ever presented.

The wonderful Outlander series that so many know so well tackles the Jacobite Rising and Bonnie Prince Charlie, and to a certain extent, paints the portrait of a stupid prince. The facts aren't necessarily all wrong. But there are various interpretations and motivations behind them as well.

To my mind, Charles was neither as good, nor as bad, as he was painted. His decisions seem to have been colored more by optimism, naïveté, wishful thinking, and pure pragmatic necessity than by lack of intelligence. And in truth, to hold together such a fragile coalition of competing goals as he found fighting beside him in Scotland, he would have needed to be both brilliant and supernaturally wily.

In 1744, he was simply still young, impatient, and hopeful. He believed in a cause he'd been carefully groomed throughout his life to embody, and he was—by nature—a bit of a gambler.

After the disappointing cancellation of the cross-channel invasion in '44, Charles and his advisors took stock of the situation between France and Britain, and the general conflicts in Europe, and they decided that the French king wouldn't be likely to launch another full-scale invasion in support of the Jacobite cause—unless he was forced into it. Given the outbreak of outright war, it was advantageous to Louis to keep the Jacobite invasion simmering and creating low-level problems for the English without diverting his own resources. But, as a gambler, Charles decided that if he himself mounted a rebellion, Louis would be forced to stop waffling and provide support.

To that end, he planned to move into Scotland the following summer, and with the help and financing of the Irish Viscount Clare—then a high-ranking commander in the French Irish forces—Charles gathered weapons and made preparations for Jacobite supporters to meet him in the Highlands. The Scottish Jacobites warned that, without thousands of French troops, this was imprudent, but Charles was convinced the French would cooperate in the end, and he'd also had a nebulous promise of help from Sweden once again.

He wasn't entirely wrong about the French. He did manage to get some French support—but it came mostly from Lord Clare, in the form of more "Wild Geese"—700 volunteers from the Irish "du Clare" brigade, consisting of men exiled from Ireland who had enlisted in the French armed forces. He also had two ships, a 64-gun formerly British warship and a 16-gun privateer vessel. The two ships were intercepted by the British, however, and both were damaged.

Only the smaller vessel with Charles aboard eventually limped to Scotland—and the weapons and most of the troops had been aboard the larger ship. By the time Charles made land in the Western Isles, he had little but himself and his advisors, the "Seven Men of Moidart," with him.

The "Seven Men" were a mixed bag of Jacobite causes. William Murray, the Marquis of Tullibardine, had been the second Duke of Atholl until the 1715 uprising, after which he was replaced as duke by his younger brother. He'd been living in exile since. Sir Thomas Sheridan was the Irishman who—along with the reviled Murray—had been Bonnie Prince Charlie's tutor. Sir John MacDonald was an Irish cavalry officer in the French forces, and another MacDonald, the Scottish Aeneas MacDonald, was a banker in Paris and the Laird of Kinlochmoidart's younger brother. There was also the Reverend George Kelly, an Irish Protestant cleric, and Francis Strickland, an Englishman from Westmoreland.

Most of these men were all well past their middle years, and few were entirely healthy. The youngest among Charles' advisors was John William O'Sullivan, the prince's friend and an Irish officer in the French forces, a battle-hardened veteran who'd experienced a brutal style of guerrilla warfare on Corsica.

You can see a bit of the problem here already. There was a lot of Irish participation among the leadership, and they were about to head into Scotland. And while there were still a few Catholic clansmen who ultimately rallied to Charles' cause, the vast majority of Charles' support there came from the clans who were Scottish Episcopal—roughly the same as Church of England—who hoped that the Stuarts would temper the majority Scottish Presbyterians, the sects of extreme Calvinism, and help to enable religious tolerance. (In the cause of religious tolerance, they were joined by the Irish.) In short, for the Scots, this wasn't just a referendum on the Jacobite cause. It was a civil war. By the time it was over, there were Highlanders and Lowlanders fighting on either sides, families split, and long-sleeping resentments rekindled.

What happened in the coming months is still polarizing today. Even now people tend either to idealize Charles or revile him. But the picture of him is seen most often from an English or a Scottish "Unionist" or "Presbyterian" perspective, and those are partisan perspectives that have been carefully shaped through the centuries. If they don't blame the tragedy of the Culloden defeat and its aftermath on Charles himself, they often blame John O'Sullivan. The fact that the Irish had an enormous stake in the Rising is sometimes minimized. It shouldn't be.

But there were other motivations at play as well. Immediately after the Battle of Culloden, the British painted the entire '45 Rising as the last gasp of the "barbaric" Highland clan system. It was never that. Though they had lost the bulk of their weapons initially, by the time they reached Culloden, the Jacobite army of 1745 had evolved into an orderly military force styled on the warfare of the European continent. And that, too, played into the "stupidity" with which Charles' actions were portrayed, both by the British and some Scots.

In the words of those closest to him, preserved shortly after the Battle of Culloden by a Scottish bishop in a remarkable collection, he was held with respect and affection. His orders were honorable, and he saw his cause as just. Here's an example from a letter he wrote to his father shortly after arriving in Scotland.

> I declare, once for all, that, while I breathe, I will never consent to alienate one foot of land that belongs to the crown of England, or set my hand to any treaty inconsistent with its sovereignty and independency. If the English will have my life, let them take it if they can; but no unkindness on their part shall ever force me to do a thing that may justify them in taking it. I may be overcome by my enemies, but I will not dishonour myself; if I die, it shall be with my sword in hand, fighting for the liberty of those who fight against me.

Back, though, to the actual events.

Charles made land in the Western Hebrides, disguised as a priest. He was scruffy and disheveled, and in the initial meetings with the Scots, he was far from what they'd expected. Nor did he have with him the thousands of French troops they'd hoped for. Still, the group moved on to

Glenfinnan near the shore of Loch Shiel, not far from where the hapless Rising of 1719 had ended in defeat. And from there, he and his supporters called the clans.

Not all of the Highland clans that had risen in 1715 came to join him. The '15 had been fresh from the Act of Union, but now the early anger and fear over the loss of nationhood had been replaced by the reality of living as part of Britain. Economically, too, Scotland would have been hard pressed to produce the numbers of fighters that had come out in the '15. Without the French troops, many of the clan chiefs saw a military campaign as a hopeless effort, and they'd seen too much hope and defeat in previous attempts, along with the harsh consequences for those who couldn't simply sail off again into exile if a rising failed. Initially, a few of the clans chose, along with other would-be Jacobites throughout Scotland and England, to take a wait-and-see approach, to gauge whether Charles had the mettle and support to take a campaign all the way.

Eventually, the ever-loyal Camerons did rise to support the cause, though, despite the nineteenth chief's earlier instance that the clan wouldn't fight without significant French support. The MacPhersons came, too, and the Macfies and MacDonnells and MacDonalds, among others.

Few of these men were well armed, though, so the loss of the French weapons was all the more keenly felt. More commonly, each clan boasted a number of armed gentlemen soldiers and a host of vassals or poor men armed with swords and shovels and picks.

Still, with these troops at his back, Charles had the beginnings of a fighting force, and he and his advisors began to shape them into an army patterned after the warfare that they themselves had learned in Europe. They soon added another important ally. Lord George Murray was the younger brother of the Duke of Atholl. He'd fought in the Risings of 1715 and 1719, after which he'd gone into exile. But he'd accepted a government pardon in 1725, and he'd come back to live on his estate in Tullibardine. Problematically, from the Jacobite perspective, he'd sworn allegiance to King George in 1739 and seemingly taken a pro-government line, so consequently, he wasn't universally trusted among Charles' advisors, and—the writings of one of his aides being among the chief exceptions—he wasn't personally liked very much. He tended toward arrogance and a quick temper. Undisputedly, though, he was bold and brave in battle, and he had a brilliant strategic intellect. If that had been coupled with conventional military training, he would likely have been the foremost military mind of the time. He also knew the Highland territory, so Charles made him deputy commander of the Jacobite forces.

Feeling a bit discouraged by the turnout overall, but still hopeful and determined, Charles raised the royal standard on behalf of his father and marched on Edinburgh with roughly 1,000 men. They captured Edinburgh with little effort on the 17th of September, and Charles proclaimed his father king. Much more importantly, as his father's regent, Charles also formally repealed the Act of Union, which made Scotland its own nation once again.

Encouraged now, the Jacobites continued the march to Prestonpans where, still with more swords than muskets, they followed the traditional method of Highland warfare with a courageous and ferocious charge against the government forces of Sir John Cope. Lord George gave Cope's troops no chance to recover from the first attack, and within ten minutes, the Jacobites had victory in their teeth.

Momentum grew. The Jacobite ranks swelled to 6,000 men and, with a fresh supply of money and weapons from France, Charles was ready to sweep into England itself. With the winds of success at their backs, he was convinced they were unstoppable.

But now the differences in motivations came into play between the different Jacobite factions.

Scotland was, at least for the moment, in Jacobite hands. They had a new Scottish king who'd done away with the hated Act of Union that had cost them Scotland. With that, the Scots among the coalition were basically happy to have achieved their objectives, and many were reluctant to press on.

The more the Scots balked at continuing, the more Charles grew obstinate. This wasn't, after all, just about Scottish independence. It was about the divine right of kings, about the throne of all Britain, about religious tolerance throughout more than Scotland itself. Right, chimed in the Irish, and what about Irish independence? Catholic rights? Fearing both that Charles had the bit too firmly in his teeth and that he was being influenced too much by the Irish— and to be fair, that he was drinking too heavily—the Scots set up a Prince's Council of twenty-odd Jacobite leaders and hunkered down for the next six weeks to debate the issue and train and arm their troops.

These were a lot of opinionated men who'd already lost a great deal. Often, choosing the Jacobite side had caused them to split from their own families, to be disowned by their parents, and to expose their wives and children to reprisal. Their lands, wealth, and liberty were at stake. They couldn't afford to risk losing unnecessarily. Tempers heated. Words were thrown around. Opinions about stupidity and courage and recklessness. There were differences of opinion between tactics as well—modern more continental-style warfare and the more traditional guerrilla style suited to the Highlands.

Charles and the Irish, desperate and convinced that they needed to keep the momentum going, pleaded their case, assured the council that the French would send support, that the English and Welsh would rise for the cause. The French envoy who had arrived with the first round of money and munitions promised, too, that a French invasion force was imminently landing in England. Eventually, the Scots agreed, and Lord George came up with a bold plan to split the Jacobite forces in two to conceal their strength and destination. The two Jacobite armies now marched off to England, where they took Carlisle and Preston in short order.

But in Carlisle, a scuffle between two Murrays—Lord George and Sir John Murray of Broughton—resulted in fresh problems. Much like Lord George himself, Broughton was a rather arrogant and opinionated man. He'd been one of Charles' initial contacts in the Highlands prior to the military campaign, and on Charles' arrival, he'd become Charles' secretary, a post he took seriously enough that he bade everyone address him "Mr. Secretary Murray" after that. He also—the charge was leveled by Lord George—insisted on micromanaging every detail of the military campaign. That same charge was also leveled at Lord George by others. With a difference of opinion at Carlisle, the two Murrays butted heads, and Lord George simultaneously clashed with the Duke of Perth, the other lieutenant general of the Jacobite army, who'd acted as the chief commander at the brief Carlisle siege. Unwilling to compromise, and unwilling to act as second to Perth, Lord George resigned as lieutenant general but ultimately emerged victorious as the newly-appointed overall commander of all Jacobite forces.

They pushed on to Derby without much government opposition.

London panicked. Literally.

The war in Europe had left the British forces weaker at home. The thought of a Jacobite invasion force sweeping through England induced a fear-driven financial crisis, and even King George made plans to retreat to Hanover if the situation worsened. But he'd already recalled his son,

William, the Duke of Cumberland, from Flanders with an army of 12,000 men, and Cumberland was heading north. General Wade, with another large army, was heading south. A Hanovarian spy in the Jacobite ranks, meanwhile, also may have started a rumor that a third army was headed in their direction.

The English Rising that Charles had promised didn't materialize, apart from one small contingent of 600 Catholics. Neither did the French landing force appear. Realizing that Charles had, at the very least, been overly optimistic and that, most likely, the French envoy had lied, Lord George urged the Prince's Council to support an immediate retreat to Scotland. Charles was despondent.

Still, morale was generally high. They'd achieved far more than they had in many years. More weapons finally arrived from France together with additional soldiers from the French Irish and Scots Brigades, and the Gordons, Mackenzies, and Frasers had also risen to join the fight. Still more French support and a large sum of gold was promised. The fresh influx of cash allowed them to pay for a few additional Lowland and English troops, and the army was continuing to transform into a modern fighting force with muskets and bayonets and a fighting philosophy very similar to that of the British troops. Their numbers waxed and waned, fighters shuffled in and out, but at most points now the army was nearly 12,000 strong.

North of Edinburgh, the Jacobite forces besieged Stirling Castle, the key stronghold near the famous battle of Bannockburn that dated back to the first Wars of Scottish Independence. The siege failed to make much progress before the worst of the winter set in, and the Jacobites retreated north to Inverness, where they needed to protect the port to maintain access to the promised French supplies. The "Butcher" Duke of Cumberland, George II's son, followed them to Aberdeen.

They all settled themselves in, waiting for the weather to improve.

Despite the French shipments they did receive, weather and a British blockade kept the Jacobites from getting the food and money they urgently needed. They'd worn out their boots marching. Desperate, they'd threatened to sack Dumfries when they went through it unless they received help and supplies, which didn't make their cause more popular.

Perhaps if the additional French gold had arrived, it could have turned the tide in their favor and avoided what came next. Maybe if they *had* continued south from Derby, they'd never have been in the position in which they soon found themselves. Or if they'd received a few more English, Scots, or French troops, the outcome could have been different. If only a few more Highland clans had risen, or if they'd chosen a different battleground . . .

If only . . .

The what ifs were endless and still endlessly debated.

Much of the blame for the coming disaster is laid at the feet of John O'Sullivan, but—like the blame heaped on Charles himself—this should be taken with a grain of salt given the personalities involved. Lord George Murray was a key factor in this, and his was a complex character, at once honorable and courageous and shrewd, but simultaneously slow to find fault in himself and quick to resent perceived mistakes in others. He seems to have had a ready eye for covering his own mistakes, and O'Sullivan made a ready scapegoat. Even among the Scots, especially those who had traveled with the prince from France and knew him best, there were many who disagreed with him about blaming O'Sullivan's character and decisions.

The conditions were what they were. The Jacobites received only another few thousand local Scots recruits.

They had, at all costs, to protect Inverness or risk losing their supply conduit—such as that was.

Cumberland's army, meanwhile, had been fortified over the winter with an additional 5,000 mercenaries led by Prince Frederick of Hesse. These Hessians deployed to cut off any hope of a southern advance—or a southern retreat—for the Jacobite forces. A further six battalions and two cavalry regiments met Cumberland's army at Cullen on April 11, 1746, and marched toward the Jacobite front guard at the River Spey.

There, they encountered 2,000 of the Jacobite forces, including the Lowland regiments, much of the remaining French regulars, the Perthshire Horse, and the remnants of the Irish cavalry that had come over from France with Charles under Sir John MacDonald. The Jacobite forces retreated to Elgin, then farther, and Cumberland's army encamped west of Nairn.

Leaving most of their remaining supplies and much of their heavy artillery behind for the sake of speed, the remaining Jacobite force hurried out from Inverness to join them and massed near the Culloden Moor.

And the leaders still hadn't agreed on what to do.

The army was too big to risk dispersing into guerrilla warfare—most of them weren't trained like that in any case, and they were hungry after the long period without supplies. Even Charles himself suffered from a fever and a condition brought on by malnutrition. Once dispersed, the troops were likely to give up and head home, or take to raiding that would turn the populace against the Jacobite cause.

John O'Sullivan, the Irish military man who'd served as Charles' quartermaster, knew this better than anyone. He advocated choosing a location where they could fight a conventional battle. A quick, decisive one, not a protracted campaign.

They didn't have much choice of where to have it.

In the forty-eight hours before the battle, with Cumberland's troops nearly on their doorstep, three sites were scouted as proposed locations. None of them were ideal. And no one "chose" Culloden Moor where they were encamped as a battleground, Bonnie Prince Charlie least of all.

John O'Sullivan rejected a recommended stand at Dalcross Castle because the short distance across the ravine would have laid the Jacobite forces vulnerable to fire from Cumberland's muskets. He suggested an alternate location,

Drummossie Moor, about one kilometer from where they'd made camp at Culloden House, where the road to Inverness was within reach to be defended. This location wasn't ideal either, but the ground was less boggy and the two wings of the army could have more easily stayed in visual communication.

The third site, proposed and preferred by Lord George, had poor ground from a tactical perspective, and the site left the road to the port of Inverness vulnerable to Cumberland's forces. The location would also have exposed the Jacobite forces to Cumberland's mortar batteries—a charge that George had himself leveled about O'Sullivan's proposed location.

Both O'Sullivan and Charles saw George's proposed site as potentially disastrous, a tacit prelude to giving up. Charles dug in his heels. Retreat was not an option—he'd already done that once retreating from Derby, and he regretted it. He was painfully aware that his men were hungry and getting weaker, leaving the whole Rising at risk of collapsing if they waited any longer to engage the enemy. The French wouldn't back him again—he knew that, too—and most of the English Jacobites and Tories, while vaguely supportive, hadn't exactly jumped up to fight for him in droves. He also recognized that he couldn't count on Scottish support for another push any time soon. From his perspective, the time was now or never.

The 15th of April was Cumberland's twenty-fifth birthday—he was nearly the same age as Prince Charlie—and his army received rations of alcohol by way of celebration. Discovering this, Lord George proposed taking advantage with a surprise night attack. They'd had great success with this at Prestonpans, moving with only moonlight to guide them, and he hoped for a repeat that would help them avoid a pitched battle after all.

The attempt was an utter disaster.

Though they had meant to leave at dusk in three separate detachments to encircle the government encampment, the Jacobite army didn't set off until well after eight o'clock.

To avoid government lookouts, they moved across open terrain. In the darkness, they made slow progress. It was almost dawn before Lord George's forces approached their destination—and they were still three kilometers out. He decided to call the whole thing off.

O'Sullivan was sent to warn the prince and the units under his command, but he couldn't find them in the dark, so two-thirds of the Jacobite army continued on to encounter the government troops before realizing that Lord George's force had retreated. Exhausted, starving after two days of not eating, and followed closely by Cumberland's army—who had woken up, well fed and rested, at five o'clock—the Jacobites couldn't hope to outrun the enemy. They fell back to their encampment and had little time to form up, much less to form an attack, before Cumberland engaged them.

What happened then was a tragedy of infighting, misinterpretation, bad terrain, and miscalculation. They were outnumbered at nearly two to one, Cumberland had them outgunned, and he got his artillery in place before the Jacobites attacked. The Jacobites failed to secure their flank at Culloden House, the MacDonalds—shifted from their customary position on the right wing—had farther to advance over difficult ground to bring up support, the Jacobite cavalry was spent, and the men were all exhausted. Bonnie Prince Charlie himself rode back and forth in front of his troops, urging them on and drawing fire, but the limited Jacobite artillery was manned by men far less experienced than Cumberland's forces, and with the main advance, Cumberland's cavalry swooped in on the flanks as the Jacobites fell back.

Recent archeology and new examinations of the battlefield and documents reveal that the overall structure of the battle wasn't fought in the previous "Highland" style of combat, which makes sense given that the Jacobite army wasn't by any means an all-Highland army. But the big, heroic spontaneous Jacobite final push led by the Clan Mackenzie and Donald Cameron of Lochiel was the stuff of Highland legend. Bagpipes wailing, knowing it was hopeless, they ran straight into a volley of muskets without firing their own guns. This was a heartbreaking glory of courage, conviction, and desperation. Speed was always critical in a Highland charge, which usually followed a smoky discharge of muskets with a full-out race at the enemy under cover of the smoke. The maneuver worked best on firm ground and a downhill terrain. Already, the clans were doubly handicapped.

And unfortunately for them, over the winter, Cumberland had been drilling his troops to counter this very maneuver. Far fewer of the government forces gave way, and although the first Jacobite line broke through, mortar shelling and superior numbers soon overwhelmed them.

The battle was over. And the "Butcher" Cumberland had no intention of giving quarter.

Heartbroken at the loss of nearly 2,000 men, Charles had to be literally dragged off the battlefield. The Irish Brigade and Royal Scots valiantly planted themselves on the road, suffering enormous casualties, to allow him and as many others as possible to escape. Behind them, the government forces were already slaughtering the wounded.

Like a Bird on the Wing

"Burned are their homes, exile and death
Scatter the loyal men;
Yet ere the sword cool in the sheath
Charlie will come again."

SIR HAROLD BOULTON
"SKYE BOAT SONG"

CULLODEN WAS THE FINAL full-scale battle fought on British soil. But the aftermath was just beginning.

In Scotland, the campaign of 1745 wasn't merely a revolution fought to restore the Stuart throne. It wasn't solely a push to end the Act of Union and throw off the yoke of the Crown in London. It wasn't only the dream of ending Presbyterian religious persecution and creating an environment of greater tolerance.

Yes, it was all of those things.

But it was also a civil war fought between Scottish people who had grown so far apart that there was fear and hatred on both sides. This was stoked by the very capable machine of Hanovarian propaganda on one side against the dream that Charles Edward Stuart had represented, a dream that was larger than life.

Before the disaster at Culloden, that dream had achieved surprising success. So much success that many people in Scotland and England had found themselves afraid that the dream would become reality. This included King George, and perhaps also his son, the Duke of Cumberland.

Cumberland, therefore, with his army comprised of English, Scots Lowlander, and Scots Highlander forces as well as Hessian mercenaries, took it upon himself to start the process that would ensure the Jacobite cause could *never* rise again. Like his father and many people in England and the Lowlands of Scotland, he saw the clan system of the Highlands as "barbaric." The Highlanders were not only "savages," they were also disloyal to the Crown, and—in Cumberland's mind—they needed to be punished.

The policies of butchery he unleashed after the Battle of Culloden were gleefully adopted by many of his soldiers, and they resulted in a spree of some of the worst atrocities and war crimes committed in any war. Worse, these atrocities continued for decades under the "Highland Clearances." Not only were virtually all wounded killed after the battle but Cumberland's soldiers killed indiscriminately. Women and children, old men, it didn't matter who they encountered in the Highlands. Many were treated as "escaping" Jacobite soldiers. If they even conceivably had Jacobite sympathies, in many cases, that was cause enough.

The 1746 Act of Proscription changed the way of life throughout the Highlands, banning not only weapons, but Highland dress and the tartan. The bagpipes were deemed a weapon of war—and no one who had heard the pipers at Culloden could doubt their power to carry the Jacobite forces forward with such extraordinarily beautiful and foolish bravery.

After confiscating a number of large Jacobite estates in the Highlands, the government next put management schemes in force and changed the way that farming was conducted. Tenant farming, a staple of clan life and culture, and a basis for the Highland economy, was replaced by crofts. So, in essence, modernization marched into the Highlands along with the Butcher Cumberland. Many of the Highland chiefs—willingly or unwillingly—went along, altering the structures of their clans and their lands to start running their own estates in the same patterns as those of wealthy landowners to the south. Many of the poor farmers and workers who were pushed out in all of this ended up becoming professional soldiers, waging war in America and elsewhere for the same government against whom they'd fought.

Prince Charles Edward Stuart and the men who escaped with their lives from the field at Culloden that day in 1746 knew none of this at the time. Charles, probably wisely, saw that there was no hope against Cumberland's force. He couldn't have known the brutality that Cumberland would unleash on the Highlands, but staying wouldn't have changed any of that.

With John O'Sullivan, Felix O'Neill, and a handful of others beside him, he picked his way to Fort Augustus on the 16th of April, and from there, with his companions ever dwindling in number, he was passed hand to hand and shelter to shelter by his supporters while being hunted by militia and Cumberland's men. He eventually made it to the lands of the MacDonalds of Clanranald, on the small island of Benbecula.

It was there that he met the heroic, twenty-four-year-old Flora MacDonald on the 26th of June, who had been recruited by the O'Neills—distant relations of hers—to help see him safely to the Isle of Skye.

The Island of Benbecula was under government control through a local militia, of which Flora's own stepfather was in command. She herself was a practicing Presbyterian and not particularly political, but at least some of the MacDonald clan were secretly Jacobite sympathizers. O'Neill asked her to get Charles over to Skye to where the chief of the clan, Sir Alexander MacDonald, had his seat.

Flora was hesitant, at first, but eventually agreed.

Almost immediately, though, troops under General Campbell were closing in on them assisted by Flora's own stepfather, and the notorious Captain Ferguson, known for his use of torture and abuse of prisoners, was searching for them by sea. Flora borrowed a dress and cloak from Lady Clanranald—who was larger than Flora herself—and they disguised the prince as Flora's maidservant, Betty Burke. Having coaxed a pass from her stepfather on false pretenses, Flora, the prince, and a crew of boatmen set off for Skye.

The courage it took for Flora to do this must have been incredible. She had to have known that, even if she managed to survive the trip, her relationship with her family, her entire life as she'd known it, was going to be ruined.

And soldiers were already waiting for them on the Isle of Skye. It took the prince's party two attempts to land safely, then Flora hid Charles in a makeshift shelter and went to find help. For many days, they picked their way around Skye and then the Prince went again from island to island, closely pursued by government troops who came harrowingly close to catching him. He found shelter with MacDonalds, MacLeods, and MacKinnons in various places, and eventually landed back on the mainland at Loch Nevis. Now disguised in Highland dress, he continued evading capture. On the long trail behind him, though, those who had given them aid were being systematically captured and taken prisoner, their homes burned or confiscated.

Felix O'Neill was captured, tortured, and after a near mutiny ensued at his abuse by Captain Ferguson, was taken to Edinburgh.

With the use of torture, and the large scale of the search, the government forces were always just behind Charles as he moved from place to place. He and his companions took to sleeping in caves and doubling back to areas where the government had already searched. And still, despite the danger, he was carefully passed from guide to guide, clan to clan, and savior to savior, sleeping on hillsides, in caverns and glens and grottos. Finally, on the 19th of September 19th, he reached Borrodale, where he found a French ship and set sail for France on the following day.

In Ireland, there's a legend that Bonnie Prince Charles— Ireland's gallant hero—was taken to France in a privateer vessel that belonged to Morty Óg O'Sullivan Beare, Captain of the Wild Geese, then hidden overnight on Dursey Island before being whisked away to France. They say Morty Óg became a privateer and a smuggler after that, supplying deserters and volunteers for the Irish Brigades. There's no indication how he got his ship, but she flew a French flag and her description is not dissimilar to the ship that took the Bonnie Prince to France.

That this is legend rather than fact, I do not doubt. But it's an intriguing story, especially given the other already dashing and swashbuckling legends surrounding Morty Óg.

Overall, the Irish mourned Charles' loss as much as the Scots, for it was their loss, too. The British propaganda didn't catch on as thoroughly there, either, and Charles wasn't vilified quite as much.

As for Flora MacDonald? After helping Charles escape, she was caught and imprisoned, and sent first to Edinburgh and from there by boat to London with the notorious Captain Ferguson. Such was her charm that General Campbell gave the captain strict instructions to treat her kindly, and by the time she had reached the end of her journey, even Captain Ferguson had written a letter to her captors asking for kind treatment for her. After a stay in the Tower of London, she was allowed a type of "house arrest" in the custody of a gaoler, and she was visited there by English Jacobites as well as by the very non-Jacobite prince of Wales. Her assertion that she would have helped anyone, even the Butcher Cumberland, who was in such distress as that in which Prince Charles had found himself, helped her to obtain a pardon in the general indemnity of 1747.

She eventually married Allan MacDonald, a distant relative, and they went on to have seven children. But with life very harsh and poor in the Highlands after the Clearances, they decided to emigrate to North Carolina, where Allan loyally served the British army in a Highland regiment in the American Revolution until he was captured. Flora's plantation was then destroyed, and her daughters violated, by American patriots, and she moved to Nova

Scotia and then returned home to Scotland, where she was finally joined by her husband. When she died a few years later, Jacobites from all over Britain came to attend her funeral in honor of the help she had given to the "prince over the water." She was laid to rest wrapped in a sheet on which Charles Edward Stuart had slept, and her gravestone left her a fitting tribute in the words of Samuel Johnson:

> FLORA MACDONALD. PRESERVER OF PRINCE CHARLES EDWARD STUART. HER NAME WILL BE MENTIONED IN HISTORY AND IF COURAGE AND FIDELITY BE VIRTUES, MENTIONED WITH HONOUR.

By helping Charles escape, Flora MacDonald allowed the Jacobite dream to live on in the hearts of many, but Charles himself never recovered from the tragedy of the end of the campaign. He died many years later, a broken man.

The Prince of Beare

"Not a ship upon the sea
Nor town nor tower upon the shore
Obeyed a chief more brave than he
Whose honored flag that castle bore,
O'Sullivan, the Prince of Beare
And Bantry of the spacious bay—
A name his foemen heard with fear,
But loved by all who owned his sway."

TIMOTHY DANIEL O'SULLIVAN
DUNBOY AND OTHER POEMS

THE BEARA PENINSULA IN County Cork, along the shores of Bantry Bay and out to the Atlantic, is one of the most beautiful places in Ireland, which is one of the most beautiful of all beautiful places in the world. This was once the seat of the O'Sullivan Beare clan, of whom two of the most famous chiefs were Donal Cam O'Sullivan, Prince of Beare, and Morty Óg O'Sullivan Beare, known as the Captain of the Wild Geese.

I write about both of these men in *Echo of Glory*, for it is their history that Meg Cameron and Niall Sullivan encounter on Dursey Island, along with some unexpected twists, as they pursue an archeological dig and discover secrets from the past as well as their own futures.

Dursey lies at the very tip of the Beara Peninsula in County Cork. It has a year-round population of three, these days, although there are three abandoned villages on the island. You can only get there by cable car or boat, and the boat is not reliable because the Dursey Sound is treacherous and moody, susceptible to racing tides and searing winds.

There are no trees on the island, either, only windswept tufted grass and gorse and heather, along with a variety of sea birds that soar above the steep-sided, ruffled cliffs.

The cable car ride takes about fifteen minutes round-trip, and there is only one car. If there are a lot of people on the island, you need to be ready to leave in plenty of time to wait through the queue to get off again.

Inside the car, there's a bottle of holy water and a copy of Psalm 91. This doesn't encourage confidence as you swing over the wild water, but the trip is—in spite of all of this—relatively easy. The car, however, smells vaguely of sheep and cow. This is because livestock has the right of way. One doesn't usually have to share with them, but you may have to wait until they've been transported back or forth.

Off the coast of Dursey, slotted alongside the main island like a piece of a puzzle, lies the smaller island of *Oileán Beag*. And on this small island is the scene of an unspeakable tragedy in the long series of tragedies that is the history of Ireland at the hands of English monarchs.

By the time this part of Ireland's history began, the Crown had made few inroads into subduing the rebellious Irish clans. Shortly following the Norman Conquest of England, they'd sent a few lords to Ireland to take up residence. It didn't take well, and English influence had drawn down to an area around what is now Dublin and a bit south along the coast. This section of Ireland came to be called the "Pale," after the custom in Europe of staking off areas that one could control and leaving all the uncontrollable, undesirable people on the other side of the pickets.

The "Old English" settlers, as the incomers (foreigners to the Gaelic Irish) came to be called, grew fairly comfortable after a few centuries. They managed a tense relationship with the Gaelic chiefs, or at least mostly kept to themselves. The chiefs and clans warred among themselves and, when they could, hit back at the Old English. Every now and then, the Old English would take more land, demand even more in taxes, impose some even more oppressive rule, rub someone the wrong way, cheat someone, or abuse someone—or vice versa—and there would be a fresh cycle of rebellion and retaliation. From an English perspective, the Irish weren't exactly "civilized," which is to say that they weren't behaving like they were *English*, and from an Irish perspective, these people were stealing their land and taking away their rights and means of keeping their families fed.

Into this environment stepped the Protestant Reformation. In some ways, the reform was less about religion—in terms of faith—than it was an outbreak of populism, a bit like we are experiencing now in many places in America and Europe. The institution of the Catholic Church, headed by the pope, had for centuries been getting more and more corrupt, failing its mission to serve the faith and help the poor and ordinary people, and leaving its clerics and officials to enrich themselves instead.

Martin Luther and John Calvin, both former Catholics themselves, had tried to change the system from within, and having failed that, they suggested maybe there was a new alternative needed—one that would help stem the widespread corruption and stop the wealthy from buying themselves salvation through the purchase of indulgences. They also wanted people to be able to read the Bible for themselves—in their own language, instead of in the Latin that very few people could understand much less read. And they decided that the pope shouldn't be the head of the church.

Henry VIII, the king of England and Ireland, had agreed with all of this. More or less. At least, he agreed with the part about the pope not being in charge.

Henry desperately wanted to annul his marriage to Catherine of Aragon. Not only did he need a male heir, which it didn't look like Catherine was going to give him, but he also urgently wanted to marry Anne Boleyn, who stubbornly refused to just become his mistress. Henry had already petitioned the pope about this, basically asking for a special ruling that would declare that his marriage to Catherine never happened.

Now the pope had a dilemma. Being Catholic, obviously, the pope believed marriage was sacred. One shouldn't, after all, simply break the solemn vow to love and honor till death you did part on a whim. He also didn't believe upsetting Catherine's Catholic parents, the king and queen of Spain, would be a good idea—not when he was already coming under pressure from reformers in Europe and needed Spain to support him. This meant he *really* didn't want to give Henry what he asked for. To get around this dilemma, the pope set the request aside for a while, hoping Henry would change his mind.

Henry, never the most patient of men, soon grew tired of waiting. And he decided—what the heck—he'd start his own religion, make himself head of the church, and give himself an annulment so he could do what he wanted. Why not? He was king, after all.

Henry thought this was a brilliant solution, if he did say so himself. And to sell it to his (Catholic) subjects, he had all that powerful Protestant Reformation stuff that was going on as ammunition. See? It's not just me, folks, *everyone* hates the pope and all that "papish" corruption. Let me give you a better, new and improved, more accountable church. Etc., etc.

Drawing on some of the same arguments that Martin Luther and John Calvin were making, he made a few minor reforms and invented the Church of England, basically—in that moment—Catholic lite. This made the transition relatively painless for a lot of his English subjects. They joined the Church of England left and right.

The Irish were more reluctant, including the "Old English" Irish, never mind the Gaelic Irish.

Ireland had always been a Catholic country. And to make things even more confusing, after Henry, whose changes had been relatively mild in England but who'd seen no problem cracking down in Ireland, the throne of England and Ireland was inherited by Henry's young (very Protestant) son, Edward V, who thanks to some pretty greedy regents who ran things in his name, was hard on Catholics everywhere. After all, in those days, if you could paint someone as truly horrible, it was easier to "legally" steal what belonged to them. Edward was followed (after a nine-day detour with Lady Jane Grey as queen) by Bloody Mary, Henry's oldest daughter, who was Catholic and didn't love all the anti-Catholic changes that had taken place, which resulted in her burning quite a few Protestants at the stake.

Into this mess came Queen Elizabeth I, Henry's second (Protestant) daughter, who—on gaining the throne of England and Ireland—decided she had better send a few more troops over to Ireland to help get those feisty Irish under control. The Irish Parliament, representing mostly the

Old English Irish, also enacted some more ugly laws against the Gaelic Irish. And based on these laws, the troops Elizabeth sent over, together with the army that was already there, were legally allowed to treat the Gaelic Irish in seriously terrible ways.

The Gaelic Irish had never been thrilled with English rule, but now they started to think just about anything might be an improvement over that. Some of the Scottish lords, like the Earl of Argyll, had been meddling around with Irish politics for a while, both on the side the Irish and on the side of stirring up rebellion. The king of Spain was all too happy to do anything he could to weaken England's position around the world. The pope, too, would have been thrilled to have Ireland remain safely Catholic. Even a few of the Old English Irish—many of whom were Catholic—within the Pale were sympathetic.

Led by the "Great O'Neill," the king of Tír Eoghain (Earl of Tyrone), along with the "Red" O'Donnell, King of Tír Chonaill, and the Maguire, king of Fear Manach, the Irish chiefs launched a revolt that came to be called the Nine Years' War, or Tyrone's Rebellion. Due in part to material support from the king of Spain, who saw the Irish conflict as an opportunity to strengthen his campaign against English colonial supremacy, interrupt English shipping, and further his fight against Protestant encroachment in Europe, it was a far harder war to win than Queen Elizabeth envisioned. By the time it was said and done, this "rebellion" cost England 30,000 men and much of the treasury, along with not a little bit of embarrassment for Elizabeth herself as the world and the men advising her looked on.

Because there were global implications, as well as her Irish interests at stake, though, Elizabeth couldn't afford to give up. She was spending three-quarters of England's annual budget to maintain and supply a standing army of 20,000—over a third more than through most of England's history to that point—with the majority engaged in fighting across the sea in Ireland.

Increasingly desperate as the war dragged on, she ordered her commanders to use any means necessary to get the rebels to lay down their arms. Mainly, this involved killing anyone who resisted, making examples of entire families, butchering livestock, and burning homes and crops as a warning and an incentive for the Irish to finally fall in line. The age-old scorched earth policy.

While this campaign of terrorism and—basically—genocide—had some effect, in some ways it made the Irish even more determined.

The pope had been supposed to send some actual troops for a while by that point, though that hadn't gotten very far. The king of Spain had sent two separate armadas to provide fighting men, but the weather hadn't cooperated and they'd turned back. Now, in 1601, he finally managed to land 4,000 men over under Don Juan del Águila at Kinsale south of Cork in the realm of the O'Sullivan Prince of Beare. Águila dug himself in at Kinsale and garrisoned the O'Sullivan and O'Driscoll castles of Dunboy, Baltimore, and Castlehaven.

Now things grew more tense. The Irish, facing greater numbers of trained soldiers under Elizabeth's commanders, had mostly avoided large, pitched battles, opting for more creative hit-and-run tactics instead. At Kinsale, though, Elizabeth's commanders sent in a force roughly double the size of the combined Spanish and Irish forces, forcing a traditional "battlefield" fight while the English ringed the Spanish position at Kinsale and laid it under siege.

The Irish fought ferociously to get through the English lines, but ultimately they were overcome by the English cavalry. The Spanish, after having held Kinsale for three months with the help of the Irish, surrendered. And unlike the Irish, to whom the English gave no quarter, the Spanish retired with their own flag flying and peacefully left under terms of truce, having agreed to also turn over the additional Irish garrisons once English troops under Sir George Carew arrived to hold them.

Most of the surviving Irish fled north to Ulster with O'Neill and O'Donnell. But some remained in Cork to continue fighting alongside the O'Sullivan, the O'Driscoll, and the McCarthy.

Donal Cam O'Sullivan Beare did two things. He wrote to the king of Spain, complaining about General del Águila's behavior and asking for new reinforcements, and he swept down to Dunboy to take his castle back before the English could get their hands on it.

With a handful of men, he snuck into Dunboy, kicked the Spaniards out, and prepared for the English to arrive in force. Knowing the battle was likely going to be ugly, he sent his family and the families of his men, along with the O'Driscoll families, 300 people in all, to his cousin Diarmuid's fortress on *Oileán Beag,* the small island alongside Dursey, with a small force to protect them.

These days, there's nothing remaining of that fort, which is the initial subject of my fictional archeological excavation in *Echo of Glory*. The placement of the drawbridge that used to span the narrow channel between the islands is still visible, and here and there, differences in the color and elevation of the grass reveal where foundations used to be. All else is gone.

At the time, though, in 1602, the fortress was thought to be virtually impregnable, protected by high cliffs and challenging seas.

And it might not have fallen, had not the English had some help.

It came down to tanistry and the interference of the English. Instead of the purely hereditary form of succession that created so many problems with regencies in England and Scotland, for example, under the tanist system, a chief was elected from among the eligible males in the line of succession. Some years earlier, when his father had died while Donal Cam O'Sullivan was still an infant, under the tanist system, Donal's brother Owen had been elected and he'd sought confirmation from English forces in Dublin. On reaching adulthood, though, Donal Cam challenged this and, again with confirmation from Dublin, become the chief in his place.

Owen, unbeknownst to most of his clan, had apparently been quietly fuming over this ever since.

As the English took their time getting down to Dunboy, the king of Spain finally sent money and more supplies, which arrived at the O'Sullivan castle on the other side of the peninsula. Donal Cam O'Sullivan went to retrieve it, leaving 143 of his best men to hold Dunboy and thinking his own family, and those of his men, would all be safe on Dursey.

George Carew sent 5,000 men and the English navy to retake Dunboy Castle.

He also received help from Owen O'Sullivan Beare, who apparently thought that if he helped the English defeat Donal Cam, they would afterwards pack up and sail off home to England leaving him in charge and in possession of Donal's lands.

Having learned from Owen of a weak spot near the main stairwell at Dunboy, the English forces began to bombard that section of the wall. After ten days of artillery fire, the walls were reduced to rubble, and under a flag of truce, Donal Cam's captain sent out a messenger to the English requesting terms. In response, the English made a show of hanging the man where those alive in what remained of the castle could see.

The remaining defenders barricaded themselves inside the cellar, which, too, was eventually breached. In the midst of bloody hand-to-hand fighting, Donal's captain tried to ignite the powder stores and blow up the invaders, but he was killed in the act. The last few survivors from the original 143 men were hanged from a single tree in the market square.

For the English, even that wasn't enough. Carew sent his forces off to Dursey Island with instructions to raze the fortress on *Oileán Beag* level with the ground.

Again, that took time and additional treachery, but they had Owen O'Sullivan there to tell them how best it might be done.

The English split their forces into three groups. One group set up Spanish cannon along the road that still overlooks *Oileán Beag*. A second group prepared themselves behind the wall of the nearby monastery that had, more than a century before, been destroyed by pirates. And the final group boarded a ship and approached from the back of *Oileán Beag*, where they lay in wait until the sea was safe enough to approach the rocks.

The three groups attacked simultaneously. The forty defenders inside the fortress fought gallantly. But they were outnumbered and outgunned.

Facing the ruin of the castle and with a score of injured within the keep already, the defenders held out as long as they could and then surrendered. Not knowing what had happened at Dunboy, they assumed at least the women and children would be safe.

That wasn't the case.

Carew's forces hanged all the remaining men. They rounded up the women and children and elderly, impaled the babies on spears and pikes and held them along in front of the crying mothers. Women were bound back to back with their children and thrown over the cliffs onto the rocks below while Carew's soldiers shot at them with muskets.

Apart from a small handful of survivors who were able to tell the tale, they killed every man, woman, and child on Dursey.

Donal Cam O'Sullivan vowed revenge. For months, he and the O'Driscolls waged a fierce guerrilla war all through the Beara peninsula, managing to take back six castles from the English forces. In the meantime, though, Carew's scorched-earth policy intensified.

Facing a harsh winter, Donal Cam O'Sullivan and the last few O'Sullivan and O'Driscoll men gathered up what remained of their families, intending to travel north more than 300 miles to meet back up with the O'Neill in Ulster. On the last, cold day in December of 1602, over 1000 people set off on foot with only a single day's supplies.

Donal Cam had plenty of money, so he didn't realize food would be a problem. But Carew and the English had been burning and destroying the length and breadth of Ireland, not only along the Beara Peninsula, so no one had food to share or sell. Pursued the whole way by the English and desperate to feed the people in his care, Donal Cam resorted to taking supplies by force. In great need of food themselves, those who owned the grain and livestock resisted.

Fighting English forces all the way north through Munster, Connacht, and Ulster, the last of the O'Sullivan allies finally took refuge with the O'Rourkes in Leitrim. Between attacks, starvation, disease, and the cold, only thirty-five of those who had set off from Beara survived the long O'Sullivan March.

But even weak and half-starved, Donal Cam wasn't finished. He continued fighting with the northern chiefs, until it became clear to Elizabeth that the cost of the war had simply been too much. Instead of demanding unconditional surrender, Elizabeth now authorized Lord Mountjoy to negotiate the Treaty of Mellifont with Hugh O'Neill. In return for surrendering, recognizing the authority of the Crown, and giving up his Gaelic title, the O'Neill kept his English title, the Earl of Tyrone, was granted a seat in the Irish House of Lords, and was allowed to keep most of his land. However, English would become the official language of Ireland thereafter, Brehon law would be replaced by English law, and the Irish earls would no longer be allowed to support the bards, the traveling poets who had thus far been instrumental in keeping Irish culture and resistance alive.

The O'Sullivan was not included in the treaty. One of the letters he had written to the king of Spain asking for assistance had been intercepted by the English. With the surrender of the O'Neill, Donal Cam O'Sullivan Beare fled to Spain and was welcomed at the Spanish court, where he had already sent his son, and the son of Diarmuid O'Sullivan of Dursey Island, as hostages to ensure his good behavior in exchange for receiving help for the rebellion.

Diarmuid's son, Phillip, became a noted scholar and documented the accounts of the survivors of the Dursey Island massacre, along with other events. His account formed a contrast to the version written by a relative of Sir George Carew.

But even then, Donal Cam O'Sullivan, the last prince of Beare, had not heard the last from the English Crown.

Queen Elizabeth had died in the midst of the negotiations for the terms of Hugh O'Neill's surrender, but that fact was kept secret for some time. James, the son of Mary Queen of Scots, united the thrones of England, Ireland, and Scotland for the first time since Robert the Bruce had won Scotland's independence. James initially accepted the terms of the newly negotiated Irish treaty, but after a failed Catholic plot to blow up Parliament—and James and his family—a punishing set of new reforms crippled Ireland's Gaelic Irish. The remaining Earls fled to Spain to seek new help, and their lands were promptly seized.

Donal Cam O'Sullivan Beare was murdered in Spain as he came out of church, and many historians believe his attacker was an agent of the English Crown.

Captain of the Wild Geese

*"No more to her maidens, the light dance is dear
Since the death of our darling O'Sullivan Beare."*

Anonymous
"The Dirge of O'Sullivan Beare"

IN 1689, IRISH JACOBITES sent 6,000 newly recruited soldiers to serve the French king in exchange for a larger force and military aid. The Irish then fought a bloody, brutal war, and in 1691, roughly 14,000 men and 10,000 women and children fled Ireland. These "Wild Geese" became King James' army in exile, melting eventually into the Irish Brigades formed earlier as a way to earn their keep. Many were O'Sullivans. John O'Sullivan was an advisor to Bonnie Prince Charlie himself, and some say that among his company there was another O'Sullivan who was a descendent of the last prince of Beare and eventually rose to become chief of the clan himself. This Morty Óg O'Sullivan was born in the wind-swept landscape of the Beara Peninsula in the shadow of his ruined ancestral family castle near Castletownbere.

The family's fortunes had long since been lost, but memories of past glories were still remembered, echoing through the ruined walls of Dunboy Castle. While he was young, Morty Óg was sent to Spain where his family still had ties, and there he received military training. After that, he fought on behalf of the Empress Maria Theresa and earned honors and a little wealth for bravery, including a fabulously jeweled sword that he brought home to Beara. Eventually he rose to the rank of colonel in Lord Du Clare's Irish Brigade.

Dressed in his uniform with gold braid on his sleeves and collar, he was as handsome as a devil and he continued to fight like one. On the road after the Battle of Culloden, he held the ground against the Butcher Cumberland's dragoons, and helped ensure that Bonnie Prince Charlie got off to safety.

He then returned to his native Ireland and kept up resistance to the British in fine Irish fashion by privateering—and by smuggling British deserters and Irish volunteers to France to keep the Irish Brigade supplied. This harassment brought him repeatedly to the attention of the government, and they soon dispatched a revenue officer to deal with the menace once and for all.

The man they sent, John Puxley, already had a long history with the O'Sullivan clan, for it was the Puxley family who had been handed the grounds of Dunboy Castle by the English after razing the castle to the ground. Puxley and Morty Óg were not disposed to love each other in any case, but there was an added enmity from Puxley's wife who didn't like that the O'Sullivan clan—and indeed everyone in the neighborhood—showed more deference to Morty Óg and his wife than they did to the Puxleys. Puxley now set out to catch Morty Óg and send him finally to prison.

Morty kept a sleek, fast ship hidden in an inlet that was known to many local men. She carried eight guns and flew the French flag, and she could outrun and out-sail most vessels in those waters, especially when she could slip behind the rocks and through the treacherous waters along the Dursey Sound.

This vessel was kept in a small inlet hidden away among the rocks of the coast, almost inaccessible except for the skilled men who manned her and knew every safe passage to the open sea. The craft, it is known, carried eight swivel guns and flew the flag of France at the masthead. Morty would gather men bound for the Wild Geese on Dursey Island where his ancestor Diarmuid O'Sullivan had once kept a fortress, and when he had enough, he would sail them away to the coast of France and come back laden with smuggled supplies. In this, he was assisted by a group of trusted O'Sullivan men and others from the area. He treated them well, and they were loyal beyond measure in return, unwilling to give him up no matter the enticement that Puxley and the Crown provided. Goaded on by his wife, Puxley found himself being made ridiculous the longer Morty Óg eluded him.

Morty Óg was away to France on the day the tragedy reached a boiling point. Denis O'Sullivan, a young cousin of Morty Óg's, made the mistake of boasting that Puxley never would catch Morty Óg—that he wasn't smart enough or bold enough to come even close. And Puxley, by now feeling much the same himself, grew even more incensed fearing that it was true. He and his party of revenuers killed the boy in a brutal fashion, then kicked his body all the way down the road to his home, where they left him in view of his horrified mother and sisters.

An old O'Sullivan matriarch then took it upon herself to march to the Puxley manor and lay a curse upon the family, their children, and any who dared to come and steal the land or livelihoods that rightly belonged to the O'Sullivans. Puxley, rather than dismissing this as the righteous ire of a woman after an atrocity, sent his men to her house where they burned her alive.

Everyone who heard this story was horrified. The O'Sullivans sent word to Morty Óg in France, and he sailed home and challenged Puxley to a duel. Puxley, whether from fear or true feeling, declined to dignify an "Irish papist" with such an honor. He then proceeded to stay out of Morty Óg's way, fearing that Morty Óg would force a fight anyway—a fight that Puxley would surely lose.

But Morty Óg would not be so dismissed. Puxley was not a religious man himself, but there were two days a year that he could be guaranteed to be seen in church. Christmas was long past, but Easter was soon upon them, and Morty Óg had only to wait and meet Puxley on his way to Castletownbere.

He then challenged Puxley again, and, egged on by his shrew of a wife, Puxley drew his gun and fired. Morty Óg allowed it, then coolly drew his own pistol and shot John Puxley dead. Mrs. Puxley set about screaming blue murder—and vowing vengeance on Morty Óg.

There were some with Morty who urged him to kill her where she stood, because they knew she would not tell the truth of who had fired first. Morty Óg vowed that, unlike Puxley, he could not kill a woman. He strode away, leaving Mrs. Puxley still screaming in the road. At that point, he continued to his own Catholic church, where he told the congregation that John Puxley would not oppress them anymore for he, Morty Óg, had shot him.

None of the congregation mourned, and none turned him in. But Puxley's wife saw to it there was a price placed on Morty's head. A price large enough to tempt one shifty man named Scully, whom Morty Óg had once refused to hire.

With his head forfeit, Morty Óg was forced to spend most of his time in France, but he had a son who continued to live, together with Morty's beloved wife, at the old house near Castletownbere. The worst happened some time later, and Morty's wife fell ill and died, and Morty Óg had to come home more frequently to keep an eye on his boy.

Scully had set himself to spy on Morty Óg, reporting him to the Crown. And once when he saw Morty's son making preparations for his father's arrival, Scully hastened to collect his reward. Forty troops boarded a fast government ship and sailed to Castletownbere, determined to catch Morty Óg alive or dead.

There was a young soldier named Harris on board, though, whom Morty Óg had once saved from some small calamity. Harris now sent his own son to the home of Morty Óg to deliver a warning about an ambush. A musket was duly fired as the government force approached the O'Sullivan house, and not knowing whether it was accident or intention, the party waved off, fearing that the element of surprise was lost.

Neither the government forces nor John Puxley's wife ever gave up searching for Morty Óg, and eventually he was caught and given a humiliating death in such ways at which the English excelled. But no man or women of Beara ever spoke a word against Morty Óg again, however much gold was offered, and Scully's name was cursed and blamed forevermore for the part that he had played.

Island Fortress

"Because now and forever more
this is where I belong to be."

DAPHNE DU MAURIER
JAMAICA INN

L IKE EMMA, THE MAIN character of *Bell of Eternity*, I grew up loving the wonderfully atmospheric, suspenseful, and psychological stories of Daphne du Maurier, including *Rebecca*, *Frenchman's Creek*, and *Jamaica Inn*, where the Cornish setting becomes a character in the story. I'm also a big fan of *Poldark*, both in novel form and the wonderful BBC series. Getting the chance to take my readers to Cornwall with a suspenseful and deeply romantic story of my own was so much fun!

Bell of Eternity is, obviously, a work of fiction. As with my other books, I connected bits of genuine history and legend with some of my own flights of fancy. I've seen the story of

Tristan and Isolde told several dozen different ways, and many different places across Cornwall claim a connection to the legend. My idea to link it to Mount's Bay, Cornwall is perhaps a little fanciful, but there is a school of thought that the man who later became St. Levan was a cousin of King Mark of Cornwall, who features in the Tristan and Isolde saga, so perhaps I'm not so very far off.

My island and castle of St. Levan's Mount is based loosely on St. Michael's Mount in Mount's Bay, a very real and magical location owned by the Lords St. Levan. Like St. Levan's Mount, St. Michael's Mount has a wishing stone and a saint who warns of shipwrecks, and there are rumors that Charles II stayed there on his flight out of England during the Wars of the Three Kingdoms. The owners held the island for the Royalists as long as they could, and fought so bravely that the approaching forces of Oliver Cromwell gave them the opportunity to abandon the island under a flag of truce and thus spared their lives.

Astute readers may notice that I have placed my island castle on the other side of Mount's Bay from the real location, on the Mousehole side instead of on the Marazion side. And because it's all fictionalized, I've renamed

Mousehole to Mowzel, which is how it is commonly pronounced.

Apart from wanting to make it clear that the story and setting are fiction, there's a reason for these geographic liberties. Mousehole was the community most impacted by the sinking of the *Solomon Browne* lifeboat from Penlee Station in 1981. Reading about that disaster—and eventually researching the tragedy of it—is what got me thinking about small communities and family traditions of service. Combined with the wisps of story connected with shipwrecks and miracles involving St. Michael's Mount, that's what provided the fuel for my island with a tradition of lifesaving that goes back thousands of years. How that connects back to Tristan and Isolde, I'll leave for you to work out.

The real heroes, when it comes to lifesaving in Britain, are obviously the volunteers of the Royal National Lifeboat Institution (RNLI). What they do is truly astounding and inspirational.

Scottish Songs

Bagpipe Music

I'M AN ABSOLUTE SUCKER for the pipes, and *Lake of Destiny* features a good few moments of piping, whether in competition, at a wedding, or a lone piper sending haunting music echoing over a Highland loch as the sun comes up.

Here are some beautiful songs you can hear on YouTube, including a few mentioned in the book. If you're not familiar with bagpipe music, bear in mind that sometimes at the beginning it takes a bit for it to get going. Most of these have the added bonus of having some absolutely stunning video or photos to watch as you listen, so it's like a mini vacation.

- Highland Cathedral, Pipes and Drums, performed by the Auld Town Pipe Band
- Scotland the Brave, performed by the Pipes and Drums of the Royal Tank Regiment
- Colonel Robertson (Massacre of Glencoe), performed by the Royal Scots Dragoon Guards
- The Gael, performed by Saor Patrol
- Dark Island, performed by Clanadonia
- Heilan Laddie, with the Royal Scots Dragoons
- Flowers of the Forest, with the Scots Guards
- Anything by the Red Hot Chili Pipers — covers of modern songs on the pipes

O Flower of Scotland

ONE OF THE UNOFFICIAL national anthems of Scotland. The words and music were written by Roy Williamson of the Corries, which commemorates the victory of Robert the Bruce at the Battle of Bannockburn in 1314, a decisive victory in the First War of Scottish Independence.

O Flower of Scotland,
When will we see
Your like again,
That fought and died for,
Your wee bit Hill and Glen,
And stood against him,
Proud Edward's Army,
And sent him homeward,
To think again.

The Hills are bare now,
And Autumn leaves
lie thick and still,
O'er land that is lost now,
Which those so dearly held,
That stood against him,
Proud Edward's Army,
And sent him homeward,
To think again.

Those days are past now,
And in the past

they must remain,
But we can still rise now,
And be the nation again,
That stood against him,
Proud Edward's Army,
And sent him homeward,
To think again.

The Braes of Killiecrankie

THE 1689 BATTLE OF Killiecrankie was the first major battle of the Jacobite Risings, a series of rebellions fought between the supporters of King James II and his descendants after the "Glorious Revolution" that deposed him and put Queen Mary and William of Orange in power.

The first three verses and the chorus were written by Robert Burns and set to an older melody. You can hear a great version on YouTube by the Corries.

Whare hae ye been sae braw, lad?
Whare hae ye been sae brankie, O?
Whare hae ye been sae braw, lad?
Came ye by Killicrankie, O?

Chorus
An ye had been whare I hae been,
Ye wadna been sae cantie, O;
An ye had seen what I hae seen,
I' the braes o' Killicrankie, O.

I faught at land, I faught at sea,
At hame I faught my auntie, O;
But I met the devil and Dundee
On the braes o' Killicrankie, O.

Chorus

The bauld Pitcur fell in a furr,

And Clavers got a clankie, O,
Or I had fed an Athol gled
On the braes o' Killicrankie, O.

Chorus

O fie, Mackay, what gart ye lie,
I' the bush ayont the brankie, O?
Ye'd better kiss'd King Willie's loof,
Than come to Killicrankie, O.

It's nae shame, it's nae shame,
It's nae shame to shank ye, O;
There's sour slaes on Athol braes,
And deils at Killicrankie, O.

MacGregor's Gathering

THE WORDS FOR THIS were written in 1816 by Sir Walter Scott, who wrote the novel *Rob Roy* about the outlaw chief and Highland hero, Robert Roy MacGregor. You can hear it sung on YouTube by Andy M. Stewart.

The moon's on the lake
and the mist's on the brae,
And the clan has a name
that is nameless by day.
Our signal for fight, which
from monarchs we drew,
Must be heard but by night
in our vengeful Halloo.
Then halloo, halloo, halloo,
Gregalach!

If they rob us of name
and pursue us with beagles,
Give their roofs to the flame
and their flesh to the eagles!
Then gather, gather, gather,
Gather, gather, gather;
While there's leaves in the forest
and foam on the river,
Macgregor, despite them,
shall flourish forever!

Glenorchy's proud mountain,

Colchurn and her towers,
Glenstrae and Glenlyon,
no longer are ours,
We're landless, landless, landless,
Gregalach landless, landless, landless!

Through the depths of Loch Katrine
the steed shall career,
O'er the peak of Ben Lomond
the galley shall steer,
And the rocks of Craig Royston
like icicles melt,
Ere our wrongs be forgot,
or our vengence unfelt.
Then halloo, halloo, halloo,
Gregalach!

The Braes of Balquihidder

THIS POEM WRITTEN ABOUT the beautiful hills of Balquhidder
by Robert Tannahill, a weaver from the Scottish town of
Paisley, has become part of the musical fabric of both
Scotland and Ireland. Set to the older tune of "The Three
Carles o' Buchanan," it also has a slightly more modern
version known as "Wild Mountain Thyme." These are part
of a musical tradition in which a man begs his sweetheart to
run away from the poor, stifling city and return with him to
the freedom and beauty of the countryside. You can listen to
a gorgeous version of this on YouTube by the Tanahill
Weavers.

Let us go, lassie go
To the braes of Balquhither,
Where the blae-berries grow,
'mang the bonnie
Highland heather;

Where the deer and the rae,
lightly bounding together,
Sport the lang summer day
'mang the braes o' Balquhither.

I will twine thee a bower
by the clear siller fountain,
And I'll cover it o'er

Wi' the flow'rs o' the mountain.

I will range through the wilds,
and the deep glens sae dreary,
And return wi' the spoils
tae the bower o' my dearie.

When the rude wintry win'
idly raves round our dwelling,
And the roar of the linn
on the night-breeze is swelling.

Sae merrily we'll sing
as the storm rattles o'er us,
Till the dear shieling ring
Wi' the light lilting chorus.

Now the summer is in prime,
Wi' the flow'rs richly blooming,
And the wild mountain thyme
A' the moorlands perfuming.

To our dear native scenes
let us journey together,
Where glad innocence reigns
'mang the braes o' Balquhither.

Loch Lomond

THIS IS ONE OF THE most familiar of Scottish folksongs. An old legend says that if a Scot dies far from home, his soul will find its way back by the low, or spiritual, road. The lyrics are first known from 1742, so it's considered a possibly Jacobite song, but the modern version is based on a printing from 1876. There's a beautiful (and fun to watch) version on YouTube by Peter Hollens.

By yon bonnie banks
and by yon bonnie braes
Where the sun shines
bright on Loch Lomond
Me and my true love
were ever wont to gae
On the bonny, bonny banks
of Loch Lomond.

Chorus

Ye'll tak' the high road
 and I'll tak' the low road
And I'll be in Scotland afore ye
But me and my true love
will never meet again
On the bonny, bonny banks
of Loch Lomond.

Chorus

'Twas there that we parted
in yon shady glen
On the steep, steep
side of Ben Lomond
Where in the purple hue
the hieland hills we view
And the moon coming out
in the gloaming.

Chorus

The wee birdies sing
and the wild flowers spring
And in sunshine
the waters are sleeping
But the broken heart
it kens nae second spring again
And the waefu' may cease
frae their greetin'.

The Massacre of Glencoe

There's a beautifully haunting song about Glencoe written in 1963 by Jim McLean. I can't reprint it due to copyright, but John McDermott and the Corries both have wonderful versions available on YouTube and elsewhere.

Scots Wae Hae

THE ORIGINAL POEM BY Robert Burns in 1793, written as
though it is a speech being given by Robert the Bruce, the
first king of Scotland following the First War of Scottish
Independence. William Wallace was the Lord Protector of
Scotland—the original Braveheart.

Scots, wha hae wi' Wallace bled,
Scots, wham Bruce has aften led,
Welcome to your gory bed
Or to victorie!

Now's the day, and now's the hour:
See the front o' battle lour,
See approach proud Edward's power
Chains and slaverie!

Wha will be a traitor knave?
Wha will fill a coward's grave?
Wha sae base as be a slave?
Let him turn, and flee!

Wha for Scotland's King and Law
Freedom's sword will strongly draw,
Freeman stand or freeman fa',
Let him follow me!

By oppression's woes and pains,
By your sons in servile chains,

We will drain our dearest veins
But they shall be free!

Lay the proud usurpers low!
Tyrants fall in every foe!
Liberty's in every blow!
Let us do or dee!

Griogal Cridhe

"BELOVED GREGOR," A LAMENT by Marion Campbell MacGregor, daughter of the Campbell of Glen Lyon, was written in 1572 after the beheading of her husband, Gregor Roy MacGregor of Glen Strae, by Grey Colin Campbell, the Campbell of Glen Orky. Years of conflict between the men had resulted in a trial presided over mostly by Campbell followers and political allies who quickly gave Grey Colin the verdict he wanted. Heavy with child, Marion was then forced to marry Raibeart Menzies of Comrie, an ally of her father's.

The original lament is long and fierce, speaking of Marion's hatred for her kinsmen for what they'd done as well as her grief for her unborn child, who she feared might not live to avenge his father. There have been many versions put to music over the centuries, so there are dozens and dozens of variations of the Gaelic text with stanzas jumbled, intermingled, and left out altogether, never mind the countless ways to translate those to English. This is one option to provide a sense of the original. There's a beautiful version sung by Mac-Talla, which you can find on YouTube with a corresponding English translation.

Many a day both wet and cold
In storms and foulest weather,
Gregor would find a rocky nook
Where we would sleep in shelter.

Chorus:
Obhan, Obhan, Obhan iri
Sore is my heart, my dearest child
Obeah Obhan Obhan iri,
Great and great's my sorrow.

Beloved of all your people,
They spilled your blood yesterday
And spiked your head on an oaken stake
Near where your body lay.

Chorus

I wish I was with my dearest Gregor
driving cattle to the glen,
Instead of with the dry old Baron
Wearing silk around my head.

Chorus

While other men's wives in town
Are at home sweetly asleep,
Here I am at your graveside
Beating my hands in grief.

Chorus

A curse on lords and kindred
who have so destroyed me,
Who caught my love unknowing,
And imprisoned him by treachery.

Bonnie Dundee

"BONNIE DUNDEE" IS A traditional folk song based on a poem by Sir Walter Scott about the men marching off with the Viscount Dundee, "Rising" to the first Jacobite call to restore King James to his throne following his replacement by Parliament in 1688 in favor of Mary and her Dutch husband, William of Orange. It became a popular cavalry march, and there's a version by the "Irish Rovers" on YouTube with scenes from the modern city of Dundee.

Tae the lairds o' convention
'twas Claverhouse spoke
Ere the king's crown go down,
there are crowns tae be broke;
Now let each cavalier
wha loves honour and me
Come follow the bonnets
o' bonnie Dundee.

Chorus
Come fill up my cup,
come fill up my can,
Come saddle my horses
and call out my men.
And it's ope' the west port
and let us gae free,
And we'll follow the bonnets
o' bonnie Dundee!

Dundee he is mounted,
he rides doon the street,
The bells they ring backwards,
the drums they are beat,
But the Provost, (douce man!),
says; Just e'en let him be
For the toon is weel rid
of that de'il Dundee.

Chorus

There are hills beyond Pentland
and lands beyond Forth,
Be there lairds I' the south,
there are chiefs I' the north!
And brave doony vassals,
three thousand times three
Will cry "Hai!" for the bonnets
o' bonnie Dundee.

Chorus

We'll awa' tae the hills,
tae the lea, tae the rocks
E'er I own a usurper,
I'll couch wi' the fox!
So tremble, false Whigs,
in the midst o' your glee,
For ye've naw seen the last
o' my bonnets and me!

Irish Songs

Óró Sé do Bheatha 'Bhaile

AN OLD JACOBITE SONG of the same title written after the battle of Culloden personifies Irelands grief at the loss of Bonnie Prince Charlie as he fled back over the sea to France. The original words were rewritten by the Irish nationalist poet Pádraig Pearse before the Easter Rising of 1916. In Pearse's version, Gráinne Mhaol has a double meaning. Literally, she is the historical sixteenth-century Grace O'Malley, the O'Malley chieftain and pirate queen (look out for my information on my book about her) who met Queen Elizabeth face-to-face and refused to bow. In the figurative sense, Gráinne personifies the spirit of Ireland returning home.

Seo Linn has a stirring version, with a rousing modern instrumental twist at the end, and Sinead O'Connor has a lovely version as well. Both are available on YouTube and elsewhere.

Chorus
Oh-ro! You are welcome home
Oh-ro! You are welcome home
Now that summer's coming!

Welcome lady who faced such troubles
It was our ruin you were imprisoned
Our fine land usurped by thieves
While you were sold to foreigners!

Chorus

Gráinne Mhaol is coming over the sea
Armed warriors as her guard
Irishmen they are, not French or Spanish
And they will rout the foreigners!

Chorus

May it please the king of Miracles for us to see
Even if we only live a week thereafter
Gráinne Mhaol and a thousand warriors
Routing all the foreigners!

Mo Ghile Mear

"My Gallant Darling" is an Irish lament written in the eighteenth-century as if the goddess Éire, representing Ireland, is grieving the loss of her gallant darling, Bonnie Prince Charlie, who has gone back over the sea to exile after the Battle of Culloden ended the 1745 Jacobite Rising. It was written in the Irish language by Seán Clárach Mac Domhnaill, and there are probably a hundred different translations.

One of the most beautiful versions of this beautiful song is sung in Irish by the University College of Dublin Choral Scholars. Sting and the Chieftains did a version of this in mixed English and Irish. Both versions are available on YouTube and for purchase elsewhere.

Chorus
He is my hero, my gallant darling
He is my caesar, a gallant darling
Neither rest nor fortune have I found
Since my gallant hero went away.

I'm filled with sorrow all day long,
My heart in pain and hot tears flowing
While he's gone off across the sea
And no news from him we know at home.

Chorus

Proud and gallant was he born
A king's son of noble mien
A fiery heart engaged to lead
The bravest follow him to the field.

Chorus

Let his story be sung while sweet harps mourn
And toasts drunk to his noble cause
With hope beating and heart aflame
To wish him strength and bring him home.

Ar Éirinn Ní Neosfainn Cé Hí

IN MY PERSONAL OPINION, "For Ireland, I'd Not Tell Her Name" is one of the most beautiful of all Irish folk songs. It's a love song of the "aisling" or "vision" type, in which a beautiful damsel in distress personifies the Irish nation or sovereignty. Maria McCool has an utterly breathtaking version available on YouTube and elsewhere.

Last night as I strolled abroad
On the far side of my farm
I was approached by a comely maiden
Who left me distraught and weak.

I was captivated by her
demeanor and shapeliness
By her sensitive and delicate mouth,
I hastened to approach her
But for Ireland I'd not tell her name.

If only this maiden heeded my words,
What I'd tell her would be true.
Indeed I'd devote myself to her
And see to her welfare.

I would regale her with my story
And I longed to take her to my heart
Where I'd grant her pride of place

But for Ireland I'd not tell her name.

There is a beautiful young maiden
On the far side of my farm
Generosity and kindness shine in her face
With the exceeding
beauty of her countenance.

Her hair reaches to the ground
Sparkling like yellow gold;
Her cheeks blush like the rose
But for Ireland I'd not tell her name.

Dirge of O'Sullivan Beare

This lament was allegedly written, sometime in the nineteenth century, by his old nurse in mourning for Morty Óg O'Sullivan Beare, the outlaw chief of the O'Sullivan Beare clan. Morty was killed for shooting revenue officer John Puxley, who just happened to be one of the Puxleys to whom the English had given the land at Dunboy castle that had once been the O'Sullivan seat. But as the legend suggests that Morty did this in revenge for Puxley having burned that same nurse alive in her house, there's a disconnect somewhere. (Which is why I didn't include the identity of the woman in my version of the legend in "The Captain of the Wild Geese.")

The sun on Ivera
no longer shines brightly,
The voice of her music
no longer is sprightly.
No more to her maidens,
the light dance is dear,
Since the death of
our darling O'Sullivan Beare.

Scully, thou false one,
you basely betrayed him
In his strong hour of need,
when thy right hand should aid him.
He fed thee, he clad thee,

you had all could delight thee.
You left him, you sold him,
may Heaven requite thee.

Scully, may all kinds
of evil attend thee
On thy dark road of life,
may no kind one befriend thee.
May fevers long burn thee,
and agues long freeze thee.
May the strong hand of God
in his red anger seize thee.

Had he died calmly,
I would not deplore him
Or if the wild strife of
the sea-war closed o'er him.
But with ropes round his white
limbs through ocean to trail him.
Like a fish after slaughter,
'tis therefore I wail him.

Long may the curse of
his people pursue them,
Scully that sold him
and soldier that slew him.
One glimpse of heaven's light
may they see never,
May the hearthstone of hell
be their best bed forever.
In the hole which the vile hands
of soldiers had made thee,
Unhonoured, unshrouded,
and headless they laid thee.

No sigh to regret thee,
no eye to rain o'er thee,
No dirge to lament thee,
no friend to deplore thee.
Dear head of my darling,
how gory and pale,
These aged eyes see thee,
high spiked on their jail.

That cheek in the summer sun
ne'er shall grow warm,
Nor that eye e'er catch light,
but the flash of the storm.
A curse, blessed ocean,
is on thy green water
From the haven of Cork
to Ivera of slaughter
Since the billows were dyed
with thy red wounds of fear
Of Muiertach Oge,
our O'Sullivan Beare.

Romantic Celtic Recipes

Apple Butterscotch Pie

AS WITH MOST THINGS historically Scottish, the origin of the term "butterscotch" is shrouded in controversy and heavily Anglicized through a long history of war, destruction of records, and the suppression of Scots Gaelic.

The Keillers of Dundee, manufacturers of the famous Dundee Orange Marmalade, may have made butterscotch as far back as 1797. The first literary reference comes from Nottingham in 1847, and a nineteenth-century article in *The Doncaster Archives* claimed that a sweet-maker there was making "butter-scotch" as early as 1817. This makes sense if the recipe was originally from Scotland and moving southward. Other sources argue that the "scotch" part of the word comes from "scorching" the syrup, or "scoring" the sweets as they cool for easier breaking.

Whatever the origin of the word, the brown sugar and butter caramelize deliciously over the apples in the baking. Add a dollop of plum jam and a meringue topping, and this mouthwatering dessert will quickly become a favorite for any romantic evening.

FOR FILLING

Ingredients:

1. Basic pastry crust (see recipe or store-bought)
2. 4-6 cups favorite pie apples
3. 1/2 cup plus one tbsp granulated sugar
4. 1/3 cup Demerara sugar (light brown)

5. 2 tbsp plum jam
6. 2 tbsp flour
7. 2 tbsp cream
8. 1 egg
9. 2 egg whites
10. pinch of salt

Step-by-Step:

1. Line a 9-inch fluted metal flan tin with pastry dough.
2. Preheat oven to 425°F
3. Peel, core, and slice the apples thin. Layer until they fill the crust completely.
4. In a small bowl, beat the whole egg with one tablespoon of cream.
5. In a separate bowl, mix brown sugar, flour, and salt.
6. Combine wet mixture with dry.
7. Spread combined ingredients over the apples in the tin and bake at 425°F for ten minutes.
8. Reduce oven temp to 350°F and bake for 20 additional minutes or until the apples are soft.
9. In a clean, dry bowl, whip egg whites at medium speed with an electric mixer until firm peaks form. Beating constantly, add granulated sugar to form a smooth, thick, and glossy meringue.
10. Spread plum jam over the apples.
11. Cover with meringue topping and use the flat side of a knife to swirl the meringue into pretty peaks.
12. Bake at 350°F for 15-25 minutes or so until the meringue is lightly golden. Chill and serve cold.

For Pie Crust

Ingredients:

1. 1 cup all-purpose flour
2. 8 tbsp unsalted butter
3. 2 tbsp caster (fine-granulated) sugar
4. 1 egg yolk
5. 1 tbsp iced water
6. 1 tbsp butter
7. Pastry weights or 1 cup dried beans or rice

Step-by-Step:

1. Coat a 9-inch pan with melted butter.
2. Sift the flour into a large bowl and crumble in the butter. Combine butter and flour until the mixture forms large crumbs.
3. Add sugar, egg yolk, and water to form a soft dough.
4. Press the dough into a ball, then roll it out between two sheets of plastic wrap, until it is 1/8-inch thick, turning frequently to get a round shape big enough to cover the base and sides of your pan.
5. Remove only one side of the plastic wrap and gently ease the pastry into the tin. Through the remaining plastic wrap, press the dough firmly into the bottom and flutes of the tin, then remove the plastic and trim off the excess at the top.
6. Vent the pastry with a fork. Refrigerate 20 minutes.
7. If pre-baking, line the crust with wax paper, distribute weights, rice, or beans evenly on top, and bake for 35 minutes.

Basic Pastry Crust

Scots love their sweets, especially cakes and pies. Called a flan case in Scotland, this easy crust can be used for traditional sweet and savory pies and quiches as well fruit-filled tarts and other desserts. Bake it in a fluted metal quiche, tartlet, or flan tin. Fill it to suit your taste!

Ingredients:

1. 1 cup all-purpose flour
2. 8 tbsp unsalted butter
3. 2 tbsp caster (fine-granulated) sugar
4. 1 egg yolk
5. 1 tbsp iced water
6. 1 tbsp butter
7. Pastry weights or 1 cup dried beans or rice

Step-by-Step:

1. If pre-baking, preheat the oven to 350°F.
2. Using a pastry brush, coat a 9-inch pan with melted butter.
3. Sift the flour into a large bowl and crumble in the butter. Combine butter and flour, rubbing together with the back of a wooden spoon for until the mixture resembles large crumbs.
4. Stir in the sugar.
5. Add egg yolk and water, and stir until the mixture forms a fine, soft dough.

6. Press the dough into a ball, then roll it out between two sheets of plastic wrap, until it is 1/8-inch thick, turning frequently to get a round shape big enough to cover the base and sides of your pan.

7. Remove only one side of the plastic wrap and gently ease the pastry into the tin. Through the plastic wrap, press the dough firmly into the bottom and flutes of the tin, then remove the plastic and trim off the excess dough at the top.

8. Vent the pastry with a fork. Refrigerate 20 minutes.

9. If pre-baking, line the crust with wax paper, distribute weights, rice, or beans evenly on top, and bake for 35 minutes.

Makes one 9-inch tart or pie crust, six 4-inch tartlets, twelve 2-inch small tartlets, or 24 mini-tartlets.

Basic Tartlet Crusts

THIS RECIPE CAN BE used rolled-out for fluted tartlet pans or pressed directly into muffin or mini-muffin tins for an easier tea dessert alternative. Fill with your choice of sweet or savory fillings.

Ingredients:

- 1 1/4 cups all-purpose flour
- 1/3 cup granulated sugar
- 1/4 tsp salt
- 8 tbsp cold unsalted butter
- 2 tbsp very cold water
- 1 egg yolk
- 1 tsp vanilla extract
- 2 tbsp butter

Step-by-Step:

1. If pre-baking, preheat the oven to 350°F.
2. Lightly coat tartlet tins or muffin pans with melted butter.
3. Sift the flour into a large bowl and crumble in the butter. Combine butter and flour, rubbing together with the back of a wooden spoon until the mixture resembles large crumbs.
4. Stir in the sugar.
5. Add egg yolk and water, and stir until the mixture forms a fine, soft dough.

6.   Press the dough into a ball, then roll it out between two sheets of plastic wrap until it is 1/8-inch thick, turning frequently to get a round shape big enough to cover the base and sides of your pan.

7.   Remove only one side of the plastic wrap and gently ease the pastry into the tin. Through the plastic wrap, press the dough firmly into the bottom and flutes of the tin, then remove the plastic and trim off the excess dough at the top.

8.   Vent the pastry with a fork. Refrigerate 20 minutes.

9.   If pre-baking, line the crust with wax paper, distribute weights, rice, or beans evenly on top, and bake for 35 minutes.

Makes six 4-inch tartlets, twelve 2-inch small tartlets, or 24 mini-tartlets.

Chicken Bonnie Prince Charlie

DESPITE A ROCKY HISTORY with the Stewart kings since James I took away their right to officially use the name MacGregor, the MacGregors of Balquhidder were staunch Jacobites, supporting every Rising from 1689 to the last failed attempt with Bonnie Prince Charlie. The recipe for the Drambuie liqueur used in this mouthwatering recipe was reportedly given to the McKinnon family of Skye by the prince when they gave him sanctuary following the disastrous defeat at the Battle of Culloden.

Ingredients:

- 4 boneless, skinless chicken breasts
- 4 apples (semi-sweet)
- 1/2 cup chicken stock
- 1 cup heavy cream
- 6 tbsp unsalted butter
- 1/3 cup flaked almonds
- 4 tbsp Drambuie liqueur
- 1/4 cup all-purpose flour
- 1/2 pinch of pepper
- pinch of salt

Step-by-Step:

1. Rinse chicken, pat dry, and pound until even thickness with the flat side of a frying pan.

2. Season chicken with salt and pepper and dredge in flour.

3. In a large skillet over medium high heat, melt 3 tablespoons of butter and heat until it begins to sizzle.

4. Add chicken, reduce heat to medium, and lightly brown on both sides.

5. Sprinkle with 2 tablespoons of Drambuie and chicken stock, cover, reduce to low, and cook for 10 minutes without lifting lid.

6. Core, peel, and thickly slice the apples. Melt 3 tablespoons of butter on low and cook apples until soft.

7. Turn heat off on chicken, but do not move from burner. Leave chicken to sit 10 additional minutes in pan without lifting the lid.

8. Remove chicken from pan to serving dish and warm in oven.

9. Add 2 tablespoons of Drambuie to pan drippings and gradually stir in cream. Turn burner to medium and heat, removing before sauce comes to a boil.

10. Cover chicken with sauce, sprinkle with almonds, and top with softened apples.

Serves four.

Corned Beef Soufflé

ALTHOUGH CORNED BEEF AND cabbage is often considered an Irish dish, it's not one that's traditionally found on an Irish table. In fact, corned beef in Ireland has a troubled history.

Because it was able to withstand transportation and storage, corned beef became popular in Britain between the seventeenth and nineteenth centuries. Not only was it consumed at home, it was sent around the world with the British navy, and it was traded to the Caribbean for food on plantations. Satisfying the increasing demand for beef went hand-in-glove with the practice of "plantation" and the punitive laws that pushed native Irish from their own fertile pastures.

Deprived of their homes and the richer grazing lands, the Irish worked long, hard hours in beef curing and packing industries, or were pushed off to farm less fertile soil, which they planted with potatoes. As cattle production became prevalent throughout Ireland, the native Irish became increasingly dependent on potatoes for food, which contributed to the Great Hunger, also known as the Irish Holocaust, between 1845 and 1849 when the potato crops failed due to blight.

With much of Ireland owned by Anglo-Irish, regardless of how much beef was produced in Ireland, it was too expensive for the majority of native Irish. Among the native Irish, it was seen as a luxury product, but it was relatively cheaper and more available in America, which helped to fuel its association with Irish-American celebrations.

Ingredients:

- 12 oz sliced corned beef
- 28 oz canned tomatoes, diced and drained
- 4 medium eggs
- 2 large onions, chopped
- 1 tbsp whole or low-fat milk
- 1 tbsp butter, melted
- 1 tsp mixed herbs (basil, marjoram, oregano, parsley, rosemary, thyme, and savory)

Step-by-Step:

1. Preheat oven to 350°F.
2. Grease a soufflé dish with melted butter.
3. Sauté the onions and herbs together until the onions are softened and translucent.
4. Alternate layers of beef, onion mixture, and tomatoes.
5. Beat the eggs with milk and pour over the dish.
6. Bake until golden with the center fully risen, about 20 minutes.

Serves four.

Cornish Pasties

CORNISH TIN MINERS USED to take these hand pies down into the mines with them when they weren't able to come up for lunch, but similar "pasties" have evolved all over the world. They're convenient and delicious, and though you can certainly make them according to this traditional recipe, you can switch them up according to your taste and imagination. Virtually anything works as a delicious filling.

Ingredients:

- Shortcrust Pastry (see Recipe)
- 1/4 cup onion, finely chopped
- 1/2 cup peeled potato, diced into 1/4-inch cubes
- 1/2 cup peeled turnip, diced into 1/4-inch cubes
- 1/2 cup rump steak, diced into 1/4-inch cubes
- 1 egg, lightly beaten
- salt and pepper to taste

Step-by-Step:

1. Preheat oven to 425°F.
2. Mix the meat, potatoes, turnips, and onions in a large mixing bowl and season with salt and pepper according to preference.
3. Roll the pastry into a cylinder for easy measuring, then divide into four even pieces. Keep your hands very cold. Roll each of the four pieces into rounds about six inches in diameter, about 1/4-inch thick.

4. Distribute the mixture evenly between the rounds of pastry, placing only on the right side of each crust.

5. Brush the edges with beaten egg using a pastry brush, then fold in half until edges meet and crimp crust closed.

6. Place the pasties on a greased baking sheet in the center of the oven. Bake until golden brown, about 40 to 45 minutes.

7. Serve immediately, or let cool and serve cold or room temperature.

Makes four servings.

Dundee Cake

DUNDEE CAKE IS A popular version of the Christmas fruitcake, but without the glacé cherries. As the story goes, it was first made for Mary Queen of Scots, who didn't like cherries in her cakes. I don't either, so this is a wonderful alternative. The Keiller's marmalade company mass-produced the cake in nineteenth-century Scotland.

Ingredients:

- 1 1/2 cups all-purpose flour
- 2/3 cup butter, softened to room temperature
- 2/3 cup dark brown sugar
- 3 large eggs
- 1 lb mixed dried fruit or raisins
- 1 cup candied citrus peel
- 1 cup whole blanched almonds
- 2 tbsp orange marmalade
- 2 tbsp good blended whisky
- 2 tsp baking powder
- 1 tsp cinnamon
- 1 tsp ground ginger
- pinch of ground cloves

Step-by-Step:

1. Pre-heat oven to 325°F.
2. Butter an 8-inch springform pan and line with parchment.

3. Sift flour, baking powder, cinnamon, ground ginger, and cloves together.

4. Cream butter and combine with brown sugar in a stand mixer and beat in mixer until light and fluffy.

5. Alternate adding one egg, then 1/2 cup of flour until mixture is well combined.

6. Gently stir in marmalade and whisky.

7. Fold in dried fruit and candied peel.

8. Add a little milk if the mixture is too solid.

9. Spoon batter into the greased pan and smooth surface with a wide knife or greased hands to level.

10. Cover with foil and bake for an hour on the center rack of the oven.

11. Remove from oven and take off the foil.

12. Working from the center outward, place whole blanched almonds gently on the surface in concentric circles.

13. Return to oven and bake for another 50–60 minutes until the cake is a deep golden brown and a toothpick in the center comes out dry.

14. Allow to cool to the touch, then glaze with sweetened milk.

15. Allow to cool completely on wire rack before removing from pan.

16. Store in an airtight container two to three days until ready to eat.

Ecclefechan Butter Tart

BUTTER TARTS HAVE A long tradition in the town of Ecclefechan near the Scottish border, which is why this is also called a border tart. It's wonderful cold but even better served warm with cream spiked with a wee dram of whisky.

Ingredients:

- Basic Shortbread Tartlet Shells (See recipe)
- 2 large eggs, beaten
- 8 tbsp butter, melted
- 8 oz mixed dried fruit or raisins
- 6 oz soft dark brown sugar
- 2 oz chopped walnuts, toasted
- 1 tbsp vinegar or lemon juice
- 1 tsp grated lemon peel
- 1/2 tsp ground cinnamon

Step-by-Step:

1. Preheat oven to 375°F.
2. Cream together butter, brown sugar, and beaten eggs, then gently stir in vinegar, fruit, and walnuts.
3. Fill tartlet shells with the fruit mixture.
4. Bake until filling is dark brown and set in the middle, about 20–25 minutes. Cover pastry edges with foil if they are baking too quickly.
5. Cool, then cover and let stand at room temperature until ready to serve.

Flaky Pastry

THE FLAKY PASTRY USED in Forfar Bridies falls somewhere between puff pastry and regular pie crust. The addition of lard gives it a distinctive flavor and a slightly different texture.

Ingredients:
- 2 cups, less 4 tbsp, all-purpose flour
- 1/8 tsp salt
- 14 tbsp butter
- 2 tbsp lard or vegetable shortening
- Ice water

Step-by-Step:
1. Combine flour and salt, and cut-in 8 tablespoons of butter with a pastry cutter or two dinner knives into large crumbs.
2. Very lightly rub the mixture with your hands to smooth out large lumps.
3. Add the ice water a half teaspoon at a time and stir gently until the dough begins to form a uniform consistency. Do not overwork or make too wet. Press it lightly into a ball.
4. On a floured surface, tap the dough lightly with a rolling pin several times to form a rectangle. Run over once lightly with the rolling pin.
5. Cut the remaining butter into small pieces and lightly and evenly distribute 1/10 of them along both sides

of the dough. Repeat down the center with 1/10 of the lard.

6. Roll the dough up lengthwise, then rotate 90 degrees, roll it out again lightly and line with another 1/10 of the butter pieces and 1/10 of the lard as before.
7. Roll up, rotate, and repeat until all butter and lard are gone.
8. Cover the dough with plastic wrap and refrigerate for at least 1 hour.
9. Roll out on a floured surface when ready to use.

Makes enough for a double crust pie or four savory pastries.

Forfar Bridie Pies

THIS SAVORY MEAT PIE in the traditional horseshoe shape is often served at weddings and christenings for luck, but its origin is controversial. Whether it was first made as a bride's treat or made by Maggie Bride, a traveling food vendor, it was immortalized by Forfar county resident, author J.M. Barrie, in *Sentimental Tommy*, the precursor to *Peter Pan*.

Ingredients:

- Flaky Pastry Recipe (see recipe)
- 12 oz lean ground beef
- 3 oz beef stock or bouillon
- 2 large eggs
- 2 tbsp butter, lard, or extra virgin olive oil
- 1/2 cup chopped onions
- 1/2 tsp water
- 1 tsp dried thyme
- 1 tbsp dried mustard powder
- 1/8 tsp salt
- pinch of pepper

Step-by-Step:

1. Preheat oven to 400°F.
2. Heat the butter, lard, or oil over medium heat in a small skillet.
3. Sauté the onions with dried thyme until the onions are translucent and soft.

4. On a floured surface, roll the Flaky Pastry dough into a cylinder for easy measuring, then split it into four equal portions and roll each into six-inch long ovals, about 1/4-inch thick.

5. In a large bowl, mix the beef with the softened onions, beef stock, dried mustard, salt, and pepper

6. Spoon equal portions of the meat blend onto the bottom half of each piece of pastry, making certain not to cross the center line, then fold in half to make a horseshoe and crimp the edges.

7. Score with a fork or cut small slits with a knife to vent and brush with beaten egg and water mixture.

8. Bake on ungreased foil or parchment paper until golden brown, about 55 to 60 minutes.

9. Serve warm or allow to cool completely.

Serves four.

Fruited Gingerbread

NOTHING IS AS COMFORTING and soul-soothing as gingerbread. It smells like Christmas and the best memories of home and family.

Add dried fruit before baking and a generous dollop of freshly whipped cream before serving, and it's an instant I-love-you for any occasion.

Ingredients:

- 3 cups flour
- 1 cup brown sugar
- 1 tsp baking powder
- 1 tsp baking soda
- 3 tsp ground ginger
- 2 tsp cinnamon
- 1 tsp allspice
- 1 tsp orange zest
- 1 tsp orange extract
- pinch of salt
- 1/2 cup butter
- 2 eggs
- 1 cup molasses
- 1 cup boiling water
- 1 cup apricots
- 1 cup golden raisins

Step-by-Step:

1. Preheat oven to 325°F, and line a 7-inch metal pan with greased wax paper.
2. In a medium pan, melt butter gently over low heat, then remove from heat and add in sugar and molasses until blended. Set aside to cool.
3. Sift the flour and dry ingredients together into a medium bowl.
4. In a small bowl, beat eggs.
5. Add both wet mixtures to the dry mixture and mix until smooth.
6. Stir in orange zest and fruit.
7. Pour into pan and bake for 60 to 65 minutes until firm to the touch.
8. Remove from pan to cool and store in airtight container for at least two days before serving.

Makes 16 squares.

Scones

PROPERLY PRONOUNCED "SKON" TO rhyme with "gone," legend has it that these tasty Scottish quickbread cakes trace their origin to the Stone of Scone, or Destiny, on which Scottish kings were crowned. Their popularity for tea at Buckingham Palace certainly proves they're fit for royalty.

Ingredients:

- 1 3/4 cups all-purpose flour
- 4 tsp baking powder
- 5 tbsp unsalted butter
- 1/2 cup + 1 tbsp milk
- 1/2 cup currants or raisins
- 1/4 cup sour cream
- 1/4 cup granulated sugar
- 1 egg
- 1/8 tsp salt

Step-by-Step:

1. Preheat oven to 400°F.
2. In a large bowl, sift together flour, baking powder, sugar, and salt.
3. Cut in the butter and rub until dough resembles pea-sized crumbs.
4. In a small bowl, combine with sour cream, milk, and dried fruit.

5. Add to other ingredients and lightly mix until well-blended.
6. Wash and dry the small bowl, then add egg and 1 tablespoon of milk. Beat until blended and frothy.
7. Liberally flour your hands and, on a floured surface, roll dough out into a 1/2-inch thick square. With a sharp knife, slice the dough into quarters, then slice each quarter into two triangles.
8. Place on greased cookie sheet, brush with egg wash, and let rest for 10 minutes.
9. Bake for 10–15 minutes until tops are golden brown.
10. Cut or break each scone in two. Serve warm with butter, jam, and clotted cream.

Serves eight.

Scotch Hot Toddy

OF ALL THE BREAKFAST TEAS, Scottish Breakfast is the strongest, possibly because originally the water in Scotland was so soft that it required additional flavor to get a good, strong cup of tea. No matter the time of day, Scottish tea pairs well with a lemon, honey, and a strong shot of Scotch.

Ingredients:

- 1 bag Scottish Breakfast Tea
- 1 1/2 oz Scotch whisky
- 1 cup water
- 1 tbsp honey
- 1 slice lemon
- 1/2 cinnamon stick
- Pinch ground nutmeg

Step-by-Step:

1. Place the tea bag, Scotch, honey, cinnamon, and lemon in a mug.
2. Add boiling water until the mug is nearly full.
3. Steep five minutes before discarding the cinnamon stick and tea bag. Sprinkle with nutmeg before serving.

Serves one:

Scottish Coffee

THE COMMON (SCOTTISH) WISDOM about whisky (from *uisce beatha*, the water of life) is that the Irish invented it and the Scots perfected it. Compared to Irish whisky, Scotch has a smokier, sexier flavor, which lends a different character entirely. The Irish will argue this point all the live-long day. Choose Scotch or Irish whisky and call your coffee by whichever Celtic country you prefer.

Ingredients:

- 1/2 oz good Scotch (or Irish) whisky or Drambuie
- 1/2 oz Cointreau, Grand Marnier
- 1 tsp Demerara (light brown) sugar
- Fresh, dark coffee
- Heavy cream to taste
- Whipped cream

Step-by-Step:

1. Pour hot water into selected glass or cup and let stand 30 seconds.
2. Empty and thoroughly dry the cup.
3. Fill the cup two within 1 inch of the whisky or Drambuie and coffee.
4. Add sugar and stir until dissolved.
5. Deflecting cream along the back of a teaspoon, add it gently so that it drifts across the top of the coffee,

sinking no more than one half-inch. Adjust to your liking.

6. Top with whipped cream.

Serves one.

Scottish Shortbread

Shortbread evolved from medieval "biscuit bread," which was made from leftover bread dough to which butter was added before baking at a low temperature. It gradually grew sweeter, too, and because butter and sugar were both expensive, it became a special occasion treat. Mary Queen of Scots was said to love a version called Petticoat Tails that was lightly flavored with caraway seeds. The name may have come from "petticoat *tallis*," suggesting the way the biscuits were traditionally cut into a circle then divided into wedges, much in the way full-gored petticoats were fashioned in Mary's time.

Ingredients:

- 2 cups all-purpose flour, sifted
- 1 cup unsalted butter, softened
- 1/2 cup sugar
- 3 tbsp superfine or caster sugar for sprinkling
- 7 tbsp (3 1/2 oz) cornstarch
- pinch of salt

Step-by-Step:

1. Preheat oven to 325°F.
2. On low speed, cream together butter, sugar, and salt until light and fluffy.
3. Mix flour and cornstarch together, then sift and fold into butter mixture. Do not over-mix.

4. On lightly floured surface, knead to form loose dough.

5. Roll dough out to 1/4-inch thick sheet between two sheets of parchment paper.

6. Following the outline of a dessert plate, cut into a round shape and then slice into even wedges, or cut shapes with a cookie cutter, or slice into even rectangles with a knife.

7. Prick the surface with a fork and place on lightly greased cookie sheet.

8. Bake on center rack of oven until crisp and golden, about 20 to 25 minutes.

9. Dust with superfine sugar and let cool completely.

10. Store in an airtight container.

Shortbread Tartlet Shells

Ingredients:

- 1 cup (2 sticks) salted butter, softened
- 1 1/2 cups all-purpose flour
- 1/2 cup confectioner's sugar
- 1 tbsp cornstarch

Step-by-Step:

1. If making pre-baked crusts, preheat oven to 325°F.
2. Cream the butter and confectioner's sugar together until smooth.
3. Add flour 1/4 cup at a time until lump-free and thoroughly mixed.
4. A pinch at a time, add the cornstarch until the dough thickens.
5. Roll the dough out in a cylinder for easier measurement, then divide into 12 uniform pieces for tartlets, or 24 smaller pieces for mini-tartlets. Roll pieces into even balls.
6. With the back of a round measuring spoon, press each ball into a muffin tin or fluted tartlet tin.
7. If making pre-baked crusts, bake until golden brown, approximately 20 minutes for mini-tartlets or 25 minutes for tartlets, or follow your favorite recipe for baking simultaneously with filling.

Makes 12 tartlets, or 24 mini-tartlets.

Shortcrust Pastry

Ingredients:

- 2 cups all-purpose flour
- 1/2 cup butter, cubed
- 3 tbsp very cold water
- pinch of salt

Step-by-Step:

1. Combine butter, flour, and salt in a bowl or food processor until it forms a coarse breadcrumb consistency.
2. Add water a half tablespoon at a time until the dough is smooth.
3. Chill in plastic wrap and keep very cold until ready to work and bake.

Special Offer

IF YOU ENJOYED WELCOME HOME, a review—even a word or two—on Amazon or wherever you purchase books online would be appreciated! You can also receive exclusive free access to my upcoming book about Grace O'Malley, the 16th century pirate and warrior queen of Connacht, as well as additional recipes, giveaways, news, and more at http://www.MartinaBoone.com/index.php/free/

Adult Fiction Available Now

THE CELTIC LEGENDS COLLECTION
from Mayfair Publishing

FORTHCOMING 2018

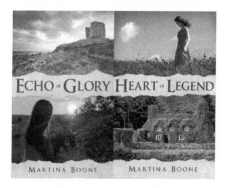

Young Adult Fiction

SOUTHERN GOTHIC ROMANCE
from Simon & Schuster/Simon Pulse

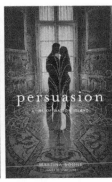

Acknowledgments

As always, thank you to my tireless editors and everyone who made this book happen, especially Erin Cashman, Susan Sipal, and my editors, Jennifer Harris and Linda Au. There aren't sufficient words to convey my appreciation.

Thank you also to the hundreds of historians and authors whose work I've relied on in writing this, especially those who have recently gone back to reexamine history in light of modern archeology and those who've gone back to the primary materials and shared the evidence that has changed my opinions of what I was taught in school.

This was never intended to be an academic endeavor, nor is it even a pure history, so I am not providing sources. That would literally double the length of this book. Again, I need to acknowledge that although the facts are here where I could find them, the personalities and interpretations that come through in the pages are my own devices, and there are many pieces of each chapter that I can only recommend you treat as a launching platform to begin your own investigations. Treat much of this as legend. Especially where human nature is concerned, legends are often truer than fact.

About Martina Boone

MARTINA BOONE IS THE award-winning author of the romantic Southern Gothic Heirs of Watson Island series for young adults, including *Compulsion*, *Persuasion*, and *Illusion* from Simon & Schuster, Simon Pulse, and of heartwarming contemporary novels interwoven with romance, history, and legend beginning with *Lake of Destiny*. She's also the founder of AdventuresInYAPublishing.com, a Writer's Digest 101 Best Websites for Writers site, and she is on the board of the Literary Council of Northern Virginia.

She lives with her husband, children, a too-smart-for-his-own-good Sheltie, and a lopsided cat, and she enjoys writing books set in the sorts of magical places she loves to visit. When she isn't writing, she's addicted to travel, horses, skiing, chocolate-flavored tea, and anything with Nutella on it.

More Information:
http://www.martinaboone.com/
Twitter: @MartinaABoone
Facebook: https://www.facebook.com/martina.boone/

WELCOME HOME

Made in the USA
Middletown, DE
15 January 2019